"And I'm going to cook something special for us, too. We can have our own party to celebrate this little miracle…"

Rafe used the tip of his forefinger to stroke Daisy's cheek. A feather-like touch but she felt it. Her face scrunched up and then relaxed again, except for one side of her mouth that was still curled up.

"Oh, my God…" Rafe breathed. "Is she smiling?"

"She heard you calling her a little miracle," Isobel whispered. "I think she liked that."

It might have only been a small curl of Daisy's lips, but it had wrapped itself entirely around Rafe's heart. He was feeling a bond with this baby that was right up there with how he felt about his own boys, and the ripple of that bone-deep emotion was including the woman who was holding this precious infant.

He found himself trying to remember something that he knew would make her happy.

"Is Mexican food still your most favourite thing in the world to eat?"

Isobel blinked. "I can't believe you remembered that. Yes, I still love it."

D0383738

Dear Reader,

Sometimes—and I love it when this happens—a germ of an idea for a story will suddenly pop into my head from nowhere. It's most likely to happen when I'm immersed in some other writing task and don't want the distraction, but I'll stop everything to make some notes because I've learned that when this happens, it's going to be a story that I will love to work on.

So there I was, working on a completely different book when a really dramatic betrayal occurred to me. My poor heroine, Isobel, might have hit a bump in the road with her romance with Rafe, but she didn't deserve to have her sister swoop in and, even worse, get pregnant from him. I could see the opening, where Belle has to come home to her sister's funeral years later, knowing that the man she'd loved and lost would be there.

I must have been in the mood for drama as I played with this idea because there's a tiny life hanging in the balance as well. Oh, and there's a twist I'm pretty sure you won't see coming!

Happy reading!

With love,

Alison xx

MIRACLE BABY, MIRACLE FAMILY

ALISON ROBERTS

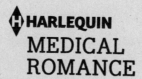

HARLEQUIN

MEDICAL
ROMANCE

If you purchased this book without a cover you should be aware that this book is stolen property. It was reported as "unsold and destroyed" to the publisher, and neither the author nor the publisher has received any payment for this "stripped book."

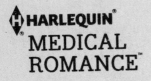

HARLEQUIN®
MEDICAL
ROMANCE™

Recycling programs for this product may not exist in your area.

ISBN-13: 978-1-335-40923-2

Miracle Baby, Miracle Family

Copyright © 2022 by Alison Roberts

All rights reserved. No part of this book may be used or reproduced in any manner whatsoever without written permission except in the case of brief quotations embodied in critical articles and reviews.

This is a work of fiction. Names, characters, places and incidents are either the product of the author's imagination or are used fictitiously. Any resemblance to actual persons, living or dead, businesses, companies, events or locales is entirely coincidental.

For questions and comments about the quality of this book, please contact us at CustomerService@Harlequin.com.

Harlequin Enterprises ULC
22 Adelaide St. West, 41st Floor
Toronto, Ontario M5H 4E3, Canada
www.Harlequin.com

Printed in U.S.A.

Alison Roberts has been lucky enough to live in the South of France for several years recently but is now back in her home country of New Zealand. She is also lucky enough to write for the Harlequin Medical Romance line. A primary school teacher in a former life, she later became a qualified paramedic. She loves to travel and dance, drink champagne and spend time with her daughter and her friends. *The Vet's Unexpected Family* is Alison Roberts's 100th book.

Books by Alison Roberts

Harlequin Medical Romance

Two Tails Animal Refuge
The Vet's Unexpected Family

Twins Reunited on the Children's Ward
A Pup to Rescue Their Hearts
A Surgeon with a Secret

Royal Christmas at Seattle General
Falling for the Secret Prince
The Paramedic's Unexpected Hero
Unlocking the Rebel's Heart
Stolen Nights with the Single Dad
Christmas Miracle at the Castle

Visit the Author Profile page at Harlequin.com for more titles.

**Praise for
Alison Roberts**

"Ms. Roberts has delivered a delightful read in this book where the chemistry between this couple was strong from the moment they meet...[and] the romance was heart-warming."

—*Harlequin Junkie* on
Melting the Trauma Doc's Heart

CHAPTER ONE

ISOBEL MATTHEWS HAD fully expected him to be here.

Her brother-in-law. Raphael Tanner.

Rafe…

Of course he was here. He would also have been here in plenty of time—not late enough to have actually missed the ceremony, as Isobel had unfortunately managed to do despite her very best efforts. When the draught caught the heavy wooden door of the church hall and made it slam behind her as she tried to close it, it was also only to be expected that he would turn, along with everybody else, to see who was arriving so unacceptably late.

What Isobel had not expected was this *awareness* of him to be so astonishingly powerful. With no more than a split second of eye contact, memories that were embedded in every cell of her body and stored away in her heart were in danger of being triggered again. She'd been so sure she was completely over this man. That she could have lived the rest of her life without ever wanting to see Raphael Tanner again. Without ever being derailed by those memories again.

That certainty had just been blown out of the water.

It was Rafe who broke that eye contact almost as soon as it happened, turning back to the priest standing beside him, but it was obvious to Isobel that he *hadn't* expected to see her here. The speed with which he looked away and the impression that every muscle in his body had just stiffened was more than enough to suggest that he might have been relieved that she hadn't shown up. That maybe she wasn't the only one who would prefer not to have memories triggered?

The pull was simply too strong for Isobel to look away quite that quickly as she took a breath and gathered her courage to face these people and this situation. She could feel her heart thumping as she registered the difference nearly seven years had made. Rafe's face was thinner and there were deeper lines from his nose to the corners of his mouth. And was he already going grey in his late thirties or was the shimmer from fine raindrops still clinging to those dark waves of his hair after being outside in the driving rain?

Isobel had noticed the still dripping umbrellas propped under the coat hooks in the entranceway of this old church hall but a lot of people were still wearing heavy coats as if they hadn't had time to warm up yet. They were also queued in front of a table laden with cups and saucers, huge teapots and an urn of boiling water, waiting for catering staff to serve them a hot cup of tea or coffee. She'd only missed the graveside part of this service by minutes, hadn't she?

Now she would have to deal with the possibility that having missed the most significant part of this funeral would haunt her for the rest of her life. That the people here would no doubt add it to their existing disapproval of her estrangement from her family. She'd known it wouldn't be easy coming here, but she had no choice but to deal with it so she might as well start by joining the end of the queue and talking to people who'd cared enough to come out in this inclement April weather to pay their respects to Sharon and

Lauren Matthews. After all, there were going to be a lot of things she would have to face in the coming days and weeks that weren't going to be easy but when they were sorted she could leave again.

And never come back.

Rafe was ushering the priest to the front of the queue to get a hot drink as Isobel joined the back. With her first impressions already gathered, Isobel could clearly read the emotion behind his features and there was enough sadness there to trigger a fresh wave of the grief that Isobel had been struggling with for days now. Ever since she'd received the shocking news of the accident that had killed both her mother and her sister.

The long, long flight from New Zealand back to England, with the addition of a mechanical fault that had kept her grounded in Singapore for thirty hours, had given her too much time to get below that first layer of grief. Time to sink into feelings of deep guilt that she'd left it too late and that any opportunity to try and repair such badly fractured relationships had been lost. There was a new, unexpected loneliness mixed in with both the grief and the guilt. The only family Isobel had ever known was gone. For ever.

This fresh wash of grief wasn't for what she had lost herself, though. This was empathy for Rafe, which was something else she would not have expected. It was, in fact, beyond disconcerting because it suggested that she cared too much about whether he was happy or not. The way her breath came out in a dismissive huff reminded her that Rafe's happiness had not been her concern for many years. It also made the woman standing directly in front of Isobel in the queue turn around.

She recognised her mother's next-door neighbour and closest friend, Louise, and saw real sympathy in the older woman's eyes.

'I knew you'd come if you could,' Louise murmured. 'Such a terrible, terrible tragedy. I'm so sorry for your loss, love.'

'I feel awful that I'm so late,' Isobel said. 'I came as soon as I could. I should have been here the day before yesterday but we got delayed. And even with this rain I wasn't expecting London traffic to be so heavy so early in the morning.'

'You're here now. No doubt you'll have time to come back here before you go away again.' Louise turned to take a step closer to the table. 'Some things are best said or done in private, anyway, aren't they? It was a lovely service under the circumstances.' She reached for a cup and saucer, already glancing towards the plates further along the trestle table, where club sandwiches, savouries and cakes were being provided as refreshments. 'I must say, Dr Tanner's done a wonderful job of organising everything. Especially when he didn't really have to, did he?'

Didn't he? What an odd thing to say, Isobel thought. This was his wife's funeral. And his mother-in-law's. The mother and grandmother of his sons. Surely nobody would have expected Isobel to have been the person to organise this funeral?

Louise was balancing her cup and saucer in one hand, reaching for a serviette and a sausage roll with the other. 'So very sad,' she added, shaking her head. 'Especially for that poor baby...'

Baby?

Isobel had picked up a cup but she didn't move to spoon coffee into it or hold it out for tea to be poured because she was still trying to process what Louise had just said. The twins would be six years old by now, she realised. Why had it not occurred to her that Rafe and Lauren would have added to their family? Maybe there was also a toddler in between the twins and…the new baby. A perfect family, with Grandma just down the road to help with the busyness of so many young children.

An echo of Rafe's voice snuck into the back of her mind.

'Once bitten, for ever shy in my case. I should be clear right from the start about that, Belle. I'm never getting married again. Or having kids. Never, ever…'

Not with her, anyway. And it still hurt that her own sister had been the one to change his mind. Even having grown up knowing that Lauren was always the favourite. Always the chosen one if both sisters were available. Even after so many years and a totally new life on the other side of the world, it still hurt and it was only natural for her gaze to roam until it found the person who had been the catalyst for that unspoken competition to have finally become unacceptable. For her life to have fallen apart. Isobel knew she'd have to talk to Rafe at some point in the next few days as she dealt with her mother's estate but this wasn't the time or place.

Rafe wasn't looking at her this time. He was still standing beside the priest and now Louise was heading towards them, possibly to tell Rafe how impressed she was by his organisation of this funeral. And Isobel found her gaze shifting to the priest because there was something a little odd in the way he was smiling at Louise or, rather, the way that smile was fading so rapidly. He was losing his grip on his cup of tea as well, the contents spilling onto the silk stole and white surplice he wore over a dark robe.

In the same instant, she could see the robe beginning to puddle on the wooden floorboards of the hall as he crumpled, seemingly in slow motion. Slow enough for Rafe to be able to put his arms out and catch the large man to at least cushion his fall.

The dramatic slump and then the unnatural stillness of the man when he was on the floor made it quite obvious that he was unconscious and Isobel's training meant that it was automatic to move in swiftly. To start doing what needed to be done to potentially save a life. Her cup and saucer clattered as she abandoned it on the table.

Rafe was already crouched over the priest by the time she got to his side. He had tipped the man's head back and had his ear close to the nose and mouth, one hand resting on the diaphragm to try and feel for movement beneath the layers of clothing, the other on the neck to feel for a pulse.

'Is he breathing?' Isobel asked.

'No.' The word was terse. 'No pulse either.'

Rafe raised his arm, clenched his fist and brought it down with a hard thump onto the middle of the priest's chest. A horrified gasp could be heard from the group of people, including Louise, who were all staring, open-mouthed, at the unexpected drama unfolding in front of them. They didn't understand that even the small impact of such a thump, if it was delivered soon enough after a witnessed cardiac arrest, could potentially have the same effect as an electrical shock in providing an opportunity for a heart to start beating again.

'Someone call an ambulance.' Rafe had his fingers on the priest's neck again, feeling for a pulse. 'Tell them it's a cardiac arrest and CPR is underway.'

With his other hand, he reached into the pocket of his suit jacket and pulled out a set of keys, turning to give them to the closest person. 'Louise, my car is parked right in front of the church,' he told her. 'Black SUV by the gate. Get my medical kit and the defibrillator out of the back. Hurry…'

'What does a defibrillator look like?'

Rafe didn't even blink. Instead of giving Louise the keys, he turned and looked straight at Isobel.

'Belle?'

By way of a response, she held out her hands to catch the bunch of keys and then turned to run to the door that led outside. She could see Rafe positioning his hands on the priest's chest now, one palm flat on the sternum, the other on top, fingers interlaced. He was starting the chest compressions and he knew exactly what needed to be done but the sooner he got his medical equipment the better. CPR alone could keep someone oxygenated and cells alive but it was not going to restart a heart that had stopped for whatever reason. Isobel increased her pace as soon as the door slammed shut behind her again, thankful she had flat-soled boots on and not heels. She could already see the big black vehicle parked by the gate so there was nothing that was going to interfere with her focus. Not even the fact that someone had called her 'Belle' for the first time in nearly seven years.

With the odds well against a successful outcome to dealing with a cardiac arrest, having it happen at a funeral was almost ironic but that wasn't even a background thought for Rafe Tanner as he kept his arms straight and continued the rapid chest compressions needed to keep this man's blood moving. With the priest being considerably overweight and the need to depress the chest by a third for the pressure to have the desired effect, Rafe was feeling the physical effort by the time Isobel came running back with both his medical kit and the small portable defibrillator he always carried.

She was panting a little from her own effort. Her boots were spattered with mud and her hair was wet from the rain that clearly hadn't stopped yet. That golden blonde hair was starting to curl. Like it always did when it got wet…

Good *grief.* Where the hell had that random memory sprung from?

He didn't have to waste extra breath on telling Isobel what to do. She was kneeling on the floor now, opening the lock on his kit. She lifted the lid and went straight for the pair of shears that could cut through any clothing, even leather shoes, but put them down to one side because they would not be interrupting compressions until absolutely necessary. With a speed that suggested the actions were pretty much automatic, Isobel grabbed some other items and wriggled herself into a position at their patient's head. She snapped a mask onto the end of an Ambu bag, tilted the man's head well back and curled her fingers under his jaw to hold the cushioned edges of the mask firmly in place. With a single nod, Rafe paused his compressions so that she could deliver two breaths. With a patient this size, it wasn't always easy to keep a perfect seal around the mouth and nose, or to push air in enough to make the chest rise but Isobel managed both with apparent ease.

'Ambulance is on its way,' someone called from behind Rafe. 'They said they'll be about six minutes.'

'Okay…thanks.' Rafe was slightly out of breath as he began compressions again but he needed to keep them up until the last possible moment when he needed to cut the man's clothing to allow the sticky pads from the defibrillator to be placed on his skin.

Again, without direction, Isobel was doing exactly what was required. She dropped the bag mask, reaching to lift the lid of the automatic external defibrillator, which made it spring to life and immediately begin issuing instructions in a calm robotic voice.

'Peel off pad labelled one and stick to the skin of the patient exactly as shown in the picture.'

Isobel had the shears in her hands and was slicing through the thick layers of the white surplice and the black robe beneath, using the fabric to make sure that any sweat was wiped from the skin. There was no need to cut the soft woollen singlet that was a poignant reminder that the priest had dressed himself with only having to stand outside in bad weather in mind, having no idea what was about to happen to him. Keeping their patient warm would be another consideration if the ambulance was delayed for some reason but

Rafe dismissed the thought for now. Just like he was easily able to dismiss any thoughts related to Isobel Matthews having suddenly stepped back into his life.

She didn't look at the picture on the pad before pressing it into place beneath the collarbone and caught up with the machine's instructions as she placed the second pad on the side of the chest.

'*Stop CPR. Do not touch the patient,*' the device said.

Rafe lifted his hands and stopped compressions.

'*Analysing heart rhythm.*'

The brief pause felt so much longer than the ten seconds or so Rafe knew it was. Especially when he was kneeling directly on the other side of the man's chest to Isobel and they'd both looked up in the same moment. When they both seemed incapable of looking away before the moment stretched into something significant because it was so much longer than you would hold eye contact with anyone that wasn't an intimate acquaintance. The faint background realisation that they were being watched, and that some of those people might well remember they'd once been an item themselves, did not seem to be enough to break this hold.

Just how many impressions and/or memories was the brain capable of producing in a space of only a few seconds? Enough for them to be indistinguishable individually, apparently, but not enough to completely blur an emotional response. And that response, which was quite surprising after all these years, included a good dollop of anger.

Why had Isobel bothered showing up at this funeral when she'd never bothered doing the right thing in the past seven years?

'*Shock advised*,' the device told them. '*Stand clear.*'

They both looked down to ensure their bodies weren't in contact with their patient. They leaned away from the patient but it also felt as if they were leaning away from each other.

'*Press the flashing orange button now. Shock delivered. Begin CPR.*'

Isobel picked up the bag mask again and positioned her fingers to get a perfect seal around the man's nose and mouth. She held her other hand on the squashy bag, ready to squeeze it when the compressions stopped for long enough. There was no point trying to push air inside lungs if they were being pressed hard from above. Rafe began counting aloud to give her warning that he was about to stop.

'Twenty-eight, twenty-nine. Thirty...' His hands were still touching the sternum but they weren't moving.

Isobel squeezed the bag but the air didn't go in as expected. She could feel it pushing out from the sides of the mask she was holding in place on their patient's face with an audible puff. She heard a shout from behind as she let the bag inflate to try again.

'The ambulance is here.'

Isobel squeezed the bag again and then realised why it wasn't working. It wasn't the chest being pressed that was working against her, it was their patient trying to breathe for himself. Rafe was also aware of what was happening. He put his fingers against the priest's neck and caught Isobel's gaze as he nodded a moment later, to confirm that he could feel a pulse.

This time, it felt very different to that uncomfortably long eye contact they'd had when the defibrillator had been analysing their patient's heart rhythm. Isobel couldn't have said whether that palpable hostility had been all Rafe's or whether he was reflecting what he'd seen in her eyes but she could certainly be confident it wasn't there this time. This was an acknowledgement between two professionals that a job had been well done. That their team work had made a difference to the world because a life had been saved.

It took all of a nanosecond to remember another shared glance that had been the way they'd met that first time. On either side of a patient in the emergency department of St Luke's Hospital, here in Balclutha. During a shift where the department was so run off its feet that the only staff available to answer the cardiac arrest alarm had been one doctor and a nurse who'd just begun working there. Rafe. And Isobel. Sadly, they hadn't been able to share the triumph of a successful outcome that time but maybe that was why Rafe had come to find her at the end of the shift. Why he'd spent the time talking through the case and reassuring her that the outcome was no reflection on her skills.

Why Isobel had fallen head over heels in love, right then and there, with Dr Raphael Tanner.

Oh, help…

She'd kept a lid on all those memories for so long but they were seeping out through cracks that had been appearing ever since she'd heard the news of that dreadful accident and had widened considerably with the emotional impact of being here at the funeral. At least Isobel found herself capable of breaking the eye contact this time. And, thanks to the arrival of the paramedics beside them, she could dismiss the memory as no more than an unwelcome passing thought.

What helped even more was that the priest was regaining consciousness. He was raising his hand, in fact, as if he wanted to push the mask away from his face.

'Hey…looks like you've done all the hard work for us,' one of them said. 'Good job, guys. Let's get him on the stretcher, get some oxygen on and then we'll get him into the ambulance and give him a thorough check.'

If anything, the rain was even heavier by the time the stretcher was loaded into the ambulance. The paramedics had been grateful for the extra help in getting a heavy patient on board, but it had still taken enough time for them to have got cold and wet. Isobel was shivering.

'You're frozen,' Rafe said. 'You should go back into the hall and have a hot drink.'

Isobel shook her head. 'I'd rather not, to be honest,' she told Rafe. 'I just need some dry clothes. I've got my suitcase in my rental car and I'll go to Mum's house. I'm hoping she's left a spare key under a flowerpot like she always used to do, otherwise I might need to wait for Louise to get home. I'm sure she'll have one.'

'I've got a key,' Rafe said. 'Just in case of an emergency.'

Of course he did. He was the sort of man who'd make sure he was always available to help his mother-in-law. Isobel kept her gaze on the flashing lights of the ambulance as it disappeared around a corner up the road. She wrapped her arms around herself as well, trying to suppress another shiver.

'I might come with you,' he added. 'I'd like to pick up a couple of things the boys left behind the last time they visited her. Then I can give you the key to keep.'

Isobel turned towards her rental car. 'You're not going to follow the ambulance in, in case they need high-level assistance?'

'The patient's stable. He's got an IV line in and he's getting oxygen and being well monitored for his heart rhythm. I know those paramedics and they can deal with another arrest, if that happens, as well as I could on the road. I'll go into the hospital later and follow up then.'

Isobel nodded. 'I expect everyone in the hall will want to talk to you.' She was biting her lip as she began walking away. 'I should also say that I'm very sorry for your loss.'

The incredulous huff of sound behind her made Isobel turn back. She could see muscles moving in Rafe's face and jaw as if he was trying to stop himself saying something. Then he appeared to take a deep breath.

'I haven't seen Lauren since she walked out on me nearly five years ago.' Rafe's voice was controlled enough to sound icy. 'I've seen your mother once in the last six months because I arranged for the boys to visit her. I'm only here to pay my respects to the mother and grandmother of my sons.'

'I'm doing this because it's the right thing to do...'

The new echo of Rafe's voice from years ago was simply another memory seeping out of that supposedly secure place. Isobel mentally tried to slam the lid shut more tightly. Starting to ask the questions that were suddenly tumbling around in her head was not going to help anything. She was here to finish things, not start anything that might complicate her permanent escape.

But he had been estranged from both her sister and her mother? What on earth had happened?

His sons? Had Lauren walked out on her children as well?

And what on earth had her mother's friend Louise been talking about when she'd mentioned that 'poor baby'?

'Do you remember the way to your mother's house?' It sounded as if Rafe was carefully keeping his tone neutral. 'Or shall I wait so you can follow me?'

'The address the solicitor sent me is the house I grew up in.' Isobel also kept her tone completely flat. 'I think I might be able to remember how to get there, thanks.'

Was Rafe just trying to rub in the fact that she'd been gone for so long? That *she'd* been the first member of her family to walk out on people? To somehow make that whole mess in her life her own fault?

Despite how miserably cold she was, Isobel straightened her back as she walked back to her car. She wasn't going to take the blame here.

Was Rafe actually not aware that what hadn't been his own fault had been Lauren's? If so, maybe that was something else that she could add to the list of things that needed sorting out before she left. It might even be a good way of finding a new lid for that box of memories.

One that was heavy enough to stay closed for the rest of her life.

CHAPTER TWO

MEMORIES ON TOP of memories.

Isobel knew these streets so well, in one of the largest towns not far from the coast in Kent. The primary school that she and Lauren had attended looked exactly the same. She could hear the echo of her beloved younger sister's demands even.

'Belle's got braids, Mummy. I want braids too.'

'Belle's got a red dress. Why can't I have a red dress?'

'Wait for me, Belle. You're walking too fast...'

Her mother's house, on Barrington Street, also looked exactly the same. Just an ordinary end-of-terrace brick house with small rooms, steep staircase and a tiny garden out the back—the sort of home a single mother with two small daughters was lucky to be

able to own. A happy enough little home to
outward appearances, perhaps, but it was obvious to everyone that it was her sister who
was the 'mini-me' of their mother. The pret-
tiest daughter. The favourite.

*'You don't need braids with your beauti-
ful straight hair. Let's give you a ponytail,
darling.'*

*'Of course you can have a red dress, Lau-
ren.'*

*'Wait for your little sister, Isobel. Don't be
so mean...'*

There was something to be said for an
overload of memories and the emotions they
could invoke, mind you. Especially when
added to the mix of grief and guilt that Isobel was struggling with. Jetlag on top of that
and it was all becoming too much. A curious
numb sensation was rolling in like a mental
fog to obscure details and muffle emotions
and make it easy to step back and simply be
aware of them in the distance—as if they belonged to someone else.

Someone who could park her car behind
Rafe's, take her suitcase out of the back hatch,
follow him up the three steps that led to the
front door of her childhood home and wait

for him to find the key and let her inside. Someone who only blinked when the door was opened and it was obvious that something was very wrong.

'What on earth is that horrible smell? Oh, my God...' Rafe had stepped inside. 'This carpet's sodden. There's an inch of water in here. No wonder it smells like a swamp.'

Isobel could hear the squelch of his shoes as he walked down the hall. She put her suitcase down on the doorstep and followed him. Her feet were cold and wet anyway and she felt so miserable that it really couldn't get much worse, could it?

'There's water coming down the stairs. There must be a burst pipe in the bathroom.' Rafe shook his head. 'It could have been leaking for the last couple of weeks. I don't suppose anybody has been in here since the accident.'

It felt as if he was glaring at Isobel. As if this too was somehow her fault.

'I came as quickly as I could,' she said defensively. 'I only got the solicitor's letter a few days ago. It would have helped if it hadn't been sent to an old work address.'

'It would have helped if someone had

known your current address,' Rafe snapped back. 'I had no other way of tracing you except to go through the police in New Zealand and I didn't think you would appreciate them turning up on your doorstep.'

The hall led into the living room that was directly beneath the upstairs bathroom. Dark smudges of mould were clearly visible on the walls and curtains. The huge bulging area of the ceiling was even more alarming, especially with water still trickling in a fast drip through the light fitting in the centre of the bulge.

Rafe stepped back. 'I didn't actually think you'd come back at all,' he added. 'Or that you'd even give a damn that your mother and sister were dead.'

Oh... Things could get worse, couldn't they?

Those words stung. Isobel could feel a wave of grief—not dissimilar to that bulge in the ceiling—ready to burst at any moment and release a torrent of painful tears. This was so unfair.

'You know why I left.' Her voice had broken edges. 'I'm sure you wanted me to leave as much as they did, to make it easier for everyone.'

'Easier for everyone or just easier for you?' Rafe had moved to peer into the kitchen. There was a lake on the linoleum and food on the bench that was covered with mould. The smell was more than simply dankness in here. 'You've been gone for more than six years, Belle. Not a word from you. Not. One. Word.'

She could deny that but what was the point? Maybe he didn't know that trying to stay in contact with her mother had only made things harder and it was hard enough to try and start a completely new life. He wouldn't want to hear about how she'd finally thrown herself into studying for a new degree and new career and how the months and then years had slipped by and how it had just become easier to put everything behind her.

'Maybe I wasn't ready to rake up the past,' she said quietly. 'Maybe I thought I had more time.'

Rafe was shaking his head again. Unimpressed. 'Well, you were wrong, weren't you? And you were wrong about something else too.' He waved his hand to encompass the destruction around them. 'You won't be staying here. It's uninhabitable.' He looked up at the bulge in the living room ceiling. 'It's dangerous, that's what it is. There's a bathtub up there that could come through the ceiling at any moment. We need to get out of here.'

He walked past Isobel into the hallway. 'I'll make some calls so that we can get the plumbing fixed and then the damage assessed. In the meantime, you'd better come home with me.'

'*What?*' Isobel almost gave an audible huff of laughter. 'Why would I do that?'

Rafe stopped in front of the obstacle her suitcase was creating, turning so quickly that Isobel almost bumped into him. She could see that the drizzle had turned into heavy rain outside now. She could also see that Rafe was angry. Or was he disappointed in her? Or hurting? Or all of the above? It twisted something inside her chest, at any rate. Another disturbing twinge that was pulling her somewhere she didn't want to go.

'To meet your nephews?' Rafe suggested, his tone impassive. 'Two little boys that have lost the mother they don't remember but that their grandmother was always telling them would come back one day because she loved them. Only she never did. They know they've got an aunty who's part of our family, but I don't suppose they believe that *she* loves them either.' He turned away to walk down the steps. 'She's never even wanted to meet them, has she?'

Isobel said nothing as she pulled the door closed behind her to lock it. That wasn't true either. She actually had a photo of the twins, when they were just a few weeks old, tucked into a pocket in her wallet. The picture that had come in the last letter she'd ever received from her mother. The one that said how blessed they all were that Rafe and Lauren had found each other.

Rafe pressed his remote and his car beeped as he looked over his shoulder. 'You might want to consider meeting your niece too,' he said.

Isobel's jaw dropped. 'So there *is* another baby? But you said you hadn't seen Lauren in years…'

Rafe had his driver's door open by the time Isobel got to the footpath. 'Oh, it's not *my* baby.' He raised his eyebrows. 'Come to think of it, I guess that, legally, *you're* her only known family.'

This was incomprehensible.

Shocking.

And Rafe must have seen that on her face because he took a deep breath.

'Look…we can't stand out here in the rain talking about this. You need to get into some dry clothes. We both do. Come home with me and I'll explain everything. If you still want to go to a hotel after that, fine, I'll help you find one.'

He was offering her a smile. Okay, half a smile but he was definitely making an attempt to be kind. Because she was his sons' aunt? Because it was the right thing to do?

Isobel swallowed hard. Her fingers were aching with cold and she could feel rain trickling down the back of her neck. Perhaps this wasn't the right thing for her to do but it felt as if she had no choice. Her world had already been spinning out of control and the new information Rafe had just delivered meant that none of it was even making sense now. She couldn't even tell if they were tears on her face or whether it was the rain. She couldn't say anything because there was a massive lump in her throat. It felt as if she couldn't even make her legs move to carry her to her car.

Rafe walked around his car to the footpath. He took the suitcase out of Isobel's hand and put it in the back of the car with an authority she couldn't begin to resist. It was, in fact, an enormous relief that somebody else was making decisions for her so that she didn't have to try and make her brain work.

Rafe opened his passenger door and met Isobel's gaze.

'Hop in, Belle,' he said quietly. 'You're in no fit state to be driving, are you? We can come back and get your car later.'

Isobel was being looked after. Being spoken to as if how she felt mattered. Being taken to a warm, dry house, shown to a bathroom and given soft, fluffy towels. Rafe put her suitcase on top of a chair and turned on the shower.

'It'll need a minute or two to get hot. The plumbing's not the best in old houses like this.'

The impressions of Rafe's house so far were a bit blurred. A huge old house in a leafy suburb. A big garden. Central heating and a nice savoury sort of smell that had to be coming from a kitchen. The house was full of comfortably worn furniture and a bit messy with toys scattered about. There was a dog too. A golden retriever that had obediently gone off to find its bed when it had been told to. It felt like a home, this house. A real family home.

Rafe pulled a string that turned on a fan heater on the wall. 'Help yourself to anything you need, like shampoo.'

Isobel nodded. 'Thanks.'

Her voice was barely more than a whisper. This was worse than that disturbing moment at the funeral when she'd realised she still cared about Rafe far more than she would have believed possible. This was more like the beginning of those dreams she used to have so long ago. Dreams when she was so much in love and knew without a shadow of doubt that she'd found the person she wanted to be with for the rest of her life. When she'd been so sure that he felt the same way and it was only a matter of time before he changed his mind about marriage. Dreams that had her cocooned in bliss only to morph into broken-hearted nightmares that she would wake from with her pillow wet with tears.

'Come and find me when you're finished.

And bring your wet clothes. There's a rack over the Aga which will have them dry in no time. I think I smelt some of Helen's vegetable soup on the go too, and it must be lunchtime by now.'

Helen?

Who the heck was Helen? A new wife? That would hardly be a surprise, would it? A man like Dr Raphael Tanner wasn't likely to stay single long. Certainly not for five years. Did that have something to do with the estrangement with her mother—his ex-mother-in-law?

Isobel had to try hard to make her stiff fingers open the zips on her long black boots. She peeled off wet tights and the rest of her clothes and stepped under water that stung her skin with the heat until she got used to it. Then she stood there for goodness knew how long, letting it rain on her head and flow over her entire body, as if it could start to wash away some of the overflow of emotion that had done her head in.

It definitely helped. By the time she got out of the shower her skin was pink and she felt warm for the first time in many hours. Her suitcase provided the comfort of well-worn jeans and an oversized oatmeal-coloured jumper that was a favourite. She towel-dried her hair but didn't bother trying to straighten the sun-streaked blonde curls that reached her shoulders. She didn't bother putting any make-up on either. Perhaps she still felt too raw to think there was any point in trying to disguise it. Or in trying to impress Rafe— which begged the question of why it would even occur to her at all.

Isobel picked up her wet clothing and set off to find the kitchen. She could still cope with everything she had come here to do. She just needed to swallow her pride and accept any help that she was offered from Rafe—the man who, as far as her heart was concerned, had cheated on her…with her own sister.

How was it that someone could have been gone from your life for more than six years but look younger than the last time you'd seen them?

Was it her bare feet? Or that huge jumper that made her look like a kid who was wearing their dad's clothing? Maybe it was just that Isobel was looking so pale. So…vulnerable…

Oh, help…was he really going to have to

fight the urge to take her into his arms and hug her? This was twisting his gut even more than seeing her standing outside her mother's house with tears streaming down her face had. He could make sure he wasn't going to give in to the urge, anyway, by using his arms to lower the clothing rack on its pulleys but a physical distraction wasn't enough to stop what was going on in his head. It would seem that he was also going to have to fight insistent memories that wanted to escape from the place they'd been banished to when he'd promised to be the husband and father that Lauren and their boys deserved.

'Here… I'll hang those clothes up.' He took the damp bundle from Isobel's arms. 'Have a seat. There's freshly made tea in the pot. I'm just heating the soup up again.'

It felt weird handling her clothes. Especially those tights. There were memories trying to surface that he hadn't allowed to see the light of day for what felt like for ever. Those intimate memories. How on earth had he ever convinced himself that that marriage was going to work? Isobel had been the one he'd been in love with, not her sister.

That was all in the past, of course, but there

was nothing like the finality of a funeral to bring things back. To make you remember things that you wished you could go back and do differently. This was a very emotional time for them both, but it had to be far harder for Isobel than for himself.

He sat at one end of the old wooden table, at right angles to Isobel because it seemed less formal than sitting opposite her. He poured himself a mug of tea. Isobel was stirring a spoonful of sugar into hers.

'This is a very nice house,' she said. 'I love kitchens like this.'

She was looking over her shoulder at the length of the room, with this old work table at the same end as the Aga and a comfortable old couch where the dog was blissfully stretched out sound asleep. There was a bench and double sink in the middle, a massive dresser stuffed with crockery beside the door leading to the pantry and a dining area at the other end of the room in front of French windows that led to the garden.

Rafe sipped his tea. 'It works well,' he said. 'I chose it because it would be walking distance to the boys' school when the time came and not far from the medical centre in Harrison Street where I work.'

That surprised her. 'Are you not working in ED now?'

Maybe it was because she widened her eyes that Rafe realised he'd forgotten just how blue they were. He hadn't forgotten it had been the emergency department where they'd first met, however. He looked away.

'Being a GP was far more practical as a single father.' Rafe wasn't about to tell Isobel how hard it had been to give up the high-pressure responsibility of running an emergency department and trauma centre that had been everything to him before his world had been tipped upside down. Instead, he let his breath out in a sigh. 'It's been a long time, Belle. Lots of things have changed.'

She was nodding. 'Of course. You're married again?'

'*What?* No…' As if he'd had the time, or the inclination for that matter, to go looking for another wife. 'What on earth makes you say that?'

Isobel seemed to be finding the colour of her tea interesting. 'I thought that's who Helen is.'

Rafe gave a huff of laughter. 'Helen is my housekeeper and she's old enough to be my mother. She's also a treasure that I couldn't do without. She comes for a couple of hours in the morning and then again after school. She also makes the best soup in the world. Are you hungry?'

Isobel shook her head. 'There's too much I need to know,' she said. 'My stomach feels like it's in too much of a knot to eat anything. But please don't let that stop you having some lunch.'

'I'm okay for a bit.' Rafe took a deep breath. 'Where shall I start? What do you need to know first?'

Isobel shrugged. 'Maybe what actually happened? All I got told was that there was a car accident.'

'There was. On the M25. It was late, dark and in filthy weather which had created surface flooding. I was told that your mother's car was overtaking a lorry. The lorry driver said they just cut back in front of him, too close. There was nothing he could do.'

'I don't understand.' Isobel was shaking her head. 'Mum hated driving on the motorway, especially in the dark. Why was she there?'

'Apparently Lauren had flown into Heathrow from Spain that evening. I guess your mother went to pick her up.'

'*Spain?*'

'That's where she's been living for the last few years.'

'Oh… I didn't know that.'

'No…'

In the silence that followed, he could sense the way Isobel was gathering her courage. She had her hands wrapped around her mug of tea as though the warmth was comforting and she didn't meet his gaze when she spoke again, questions tumbling out.

'But why did she leave in the first place, Rafe? How could she have left her kids? How old is this new baby and who's the father? I don't understand any of this.'

Oddly, seeing the brave set to Isobel's shoulders and the way she pressed her lips together so hard after asking her questions made her seem even more vulnerable. She was preparing to face whatever was coming and he had the power to make that a whole lot harder if he wanted to. To hurt her, perhaps, by telling her that he wished he'd never met any member of her disastrous family?

Except that wasn't entirely true, was it? And hurting her was actually the last thing that Rafe wanted to do. It felt like the urge to protect this woman was resurfacing from where it had been hiding somewhere very deep. It seemed like it hadn't lost any of its strength either.

'You told me something about Lauren once,' he said quietly. 'That she always got bored when she got what she wanted and then she needed to find something else. She got bored being a wife and mother. She ran off to Spain with her Pilates instructor. That didn't last but she loved the lifestyle there. Maybe she decided to come home because of the baby.' Rafe shrugged. 'I guess she knew her mother would help, no matter how much trouble she was in.'

Isobel's half smile was wry. 'Yeah…that was the way it always worked.'

'So that was when the accident happened. Your mother had gone to the airport to collect Lauren and they never made it home. Your mother died instantly.' Rafe swallowed. 'I'm so sorry, Belle. I know it was never an easy relationship, but that can make things harder in some ways.'

Her head was dipped but it didn't hide the single tear that trickled down the side of her nose. Rafe put his hand over hers and she didn't move away.

'Lauren was badly injured but still alive when the paramedics got there. They airlifted her to the ED at St Luke's but there was no chance of saving her. She had a traumatic injury to her aorta that ended up rupturing. They did everything they could but, in the end, they made the call to try and save her baby and performed a post-mortem Caesarean in the ED.'

'Oh, my God...' Isobel probably didn't realise how hard she was gripping his hand. 'She was *pregnant*? I assumed she'd already had the baby. How far along was she? And was she, I mean, is she...?'

Rafe knew exactly what those unfinished questions were about. Was the baby even likely to survive?

'She seems to be doing well,' Rafe told her. 'She's tiny, of course. They estimated the gestation to be twenty-eight weeks. She weighed one and a half kilos at birth—three and a half pounds—but she's dropped a bit since, which is normal. She was on a ventilator for a few days and is on CPAP now but being weaned off. She'll probably be in the Neonatal ICU until close to what would have been her original birth date, which will be another eight or nine weeks now.'

Isobel seemed to be hanging on every word he was saying, her eyes full of the same conflicting emotions that Rafe had experienced himself ever since he'd learned about the birth of this baby. Horror due to the tragedy surrounding the birth and the risk of it not being successful. Sadness for the tiny, helpless creature who was arriving in the world and having to fight for survival totally alone. But there was hope to be felt as well, because this baby girl *was* fighting and surviving and it was a bit of a miracle.

'There's no sign of any brain bleed, which is always a risk with preemies,' he added. 'She had a scan at seven days which was clear. And the paramedics and ED staff knew they were dealing with a pregnant woman so made keeping her oxygen levels up an absolute priority.'

Isobel was still staring at him. 'What's going to happen to her?'

It was easy to let go of her hand now. All

he needed to do was reach for his mug of tea. 'There's plenty of time for decisions to be made. In the meantime, I've taken guardianship because I'm the father of her only known relatives—her half-brothers.'

'So that's why you know so much about her?'

'Yeah. Plus, I'm visiting her every day.'

Isobel was silent for a long moment. He could hear her taking a deep breath. He could almost feel the hesitation, as if she really wanted to know more but didn't want to be involved?

'Does…does she have a name?'

'Not yet. Maybe you'd like to think of one, what with her being your niece?'

Rafe stood up and turned away before he could see her reaction that could well make him feel guilty for reminding her that she *was* involved, whether she liked it or not. Besides, Isobel might not feel like eating but it had been too long since breakfast for him. He went to the Aga and ladled some of the soup into a bowl. Then he cut a thick slice of the sourdough loaf beneath a tea towel on the bread board. He had torn a chunk of bread off to dip into his soup as he turned back to the table.

'Are you sure you wouldn't like to try some? It's really good.'

But Isobel had her face in her hands and she simply shook her head. Rafe could see a faint shudder run through her body which couldn't be due to cold because this room was overheated, if anything, thanks to the stove. It was more likely to be that Isobel was crying. Or trying not to, as she processed a tsunami of highly emotional information.

He put his bowl and slice of bread down on the table, letting his breath out in another sigh. He didn't want to feel this sorry for Isobel. He certainly didn't want to have to grapple with the urge to comfort or protect her. If he was totally honest, he didn't actually want her here, in his home, either.

But there it was. She was here and he was feeling it all, spiced up by being peppered with unavoidable memories.

'Did you sleep on the plane?'

She shook her head again.

'And you've been travelling how long?'

'About sixty hours, give or take, thanks to a big delay at Singapore Airport.'

And she'd had to walk straight into the aftermath of the funeral. It didn't matter how much distance there'd been between Isobel and her mother and sister in the end, they were her family and she had to be devastated at this loss.

Rafe touched her shoulder, waiting for her to look up and confirm what he was thinking.

'You have to sleep,' he told her. 'Doctor's orders. Before you fall over completely. As soon as I've had some lunch, I'm going to go into the hospital to see how our patient is doing and to visit the baby. I'm picking the boys up from school after that but I'll make sure they're not rowdy. You can sleep as long as you need to.'

He could see the irresistible pull that Isobel was feeling towards the prospect of a temporary reprieve. Escape from something so big, she had no idea how to start dealing with it.

Rafe held her gaze. He couldn't summon a smile but perhaps he could make his tone gentle enough to have a similar effect?

'Come on. I'll show you your room.'

CHAPTER THREE

ISOBEL SLEPT THE clock around. And then she slept some more. Such a deep sleep that she couldn't have roused herself if she'd tried but not deep enough to keep dreams at bay.

Dreams that had no basis in reality, like one in which she was holding a newborn baby, with its umbilical cord trailing, as she ran through a vast house with increasing desperation, trying to find the room where the baby belonged—where it needed to be to survive. And dreams that were too close to reality, where she was back at that fateful hospital Christmas party searching the crowd to find Rafe, who'd promised to be there but he wasn't. Going to his apartment and letting herself in because he'd just given her a key. Finding empty champagne bottles in the living room and finding Rafe in his bedroom... with her sister...

There'd been snatches of that horrible final conversation days after she'd fled that scene.

'She told me you were with Michael.'

'I was with Michael—in Resus—I couldn't leave work on time.'

'But I'd seen him yesterday...kissing you.'

'He had mistletoe. He was kissing everybody.'

'Lauren said you'd moved on. That you were happy we'd broken up.'

'And you believed her?'

'You know why...'

'I'm not your ex-wife, Rafe. What I can't get my head around is that you not only believed her—you went to bed with her!'

'I don't even remember how that happened. It's never going to happen again, that's for sure. I know how stupid it was.'

'It was unforgivable. That's what it was. It's really over now, Rafe. I just wish it had never begun. You know what? You and Lauren deserve each other. Good luck with that...'

Perhaps it was the dream that combined everything—where she was holding newborn twins as she confronted the betrayal of her boyfriend and her own sister—that finally made it possible for Isobel to escape into wakefulness. Even then, she had to lie there for a long time, waiting for her heart rate to settle and the dark cloud of the dream to evaporate completely.

The betrayal had been undeniably crushing but it was all in the past and she'd realised many years ago that looking back was never going to help her move forward, it would probably only trip her up. Yesterday's exhaustion, both emotional and physical, on top of actually being in Rafe's company had made it impossible not to look back, which explained the disturbing dreams, but Isobel *had* moved on and being here was only temporary. She could find a hotel today and get on with sorting the disaster her mother's house had become.

More urgently, she needed to use the en suite bathroom this bedroom provided. Then she had to stare at the screen of her phone for ages, making a considerable mental effort to remember time zones and why it was still completely dark outside, to get her head around the fact that she'd slept for such an unbelievably long time and it was now just after six o'clock in the morning, local time.

Too wide awake now to lie in bed any longer, Isobel got dressed in the same clothes she'd been wearing yesterday afternoon. It was also too long since she'd had a hot drink and the thought of coffee was irresistible. If she was quiet enough, perhaps she could use the kitchen without disturbing anyone else in the house?

The dog was in the kitchen, but he just thumped his tail on the cushions of the couch and went back to sleep. Isobel had never used an Aga but there was an electric jug to boil some water, a jar of instant coffee on the bench and milk in an enormous refrigerator that was stacked with an impressive amount of food. It was the two clear boxes with snap-lock lids that caught her eye on the shelves first, though, because she could see the sand-wiches inside them, along with an apple and carrot sticks and what looked like a home-baked biscuit.

School lunches.

Two identical school lunches that belonged to her two identical nephews. Rafe and Lauren's children, Oscar and Josh.

Oh, boy…she needed coffee to stop that mental fog rolling back in to cushion things that she had to face, preferably sooner rather than later. Isobel spooned a generous amount of coffee into a mug she took from a hook under the first shelf of an old hutch dresser. She added water and milk and some brown sugar from a bowl on the table. She intended to add the sugar anyway, but the loaded spoon shook and then emptied itself onto the table when she heard a small voice behind her, speaking in a stage whisper.

'That's *her*, isn't it? Belle?'

Oh, help...she wasn't ready for this. Isobel put the spoon down and started trying to sweep up the sugar granules in front of her with her hand, pretending not to have heard anything.

But then there was another voice.

'We know it is, Josh. She's our *aunty*.'

'I know that. Daddy told us. She's Aunty Belle.'

Aunty Belle. Did it sound so natural because it was so similar to Isobel? It made her smile at any rate, as she looked towards the door.

'Hey...you must be Oscar and Josh.'

The boys gave up hiding in the hallway and seemed to explode into the kitchen. The dog leapt off the couch to greet them.

'But which of us is which?' one of the boys demanded. 'Bet you can't tell.'

Of course she couldn't tell. Not only did they look identical, she'd never met them before. What she could tell, instantly, was that these children, in their matching dinosaur pyjamas, were just gorgeous. They had curly dark hair and brown eyes like their father but, unlike Rafe, they had big, welcoming smiles that held no hint of any reason not to like her.

'You're Josh,' Isobel said confidently.

He looked crestfallen. 'But how did you know?'

'I just guessed,' Isobel confessed. 'I had a fifty per cent chance of being right.'

'You've made a mess.' It was Oscar who was pointing to the table.

'I know.'

'When we make a mess, we're s'posed to clean it up by ourselves.'

Isobel nodded. 'That's a great rule. I was just about to do that.'

The dog was sitting in front of the boys, wagging his tail. And then he barked.

'Cheddar wants his breakfast.'

'Cheddar?'

'He's yellow,' Josh explained kindly. 'Like cheese.'

This time, Isobel didn't only smile, she actually laughed. 'That's a brilliant name. I love it.'

'Will you give him his breakfast?'

'Um… I don't know what he has for breakfast.'

'Biscuits. And a bit of our porridge. Are you going to make our porridge?'

'Um…'

'I have golden syrup on mine,' Oscar told her.

'And I have sprinkles,' Josh added. 'Hundreds and millions. Because they're pretty when you stir them with your spoon.'

'I'm not sure I know where the porridge is,' Isobel said cautiously.

'I'll show you.' Oscar took hold of Isobel's hand.

'No… I'll show her.' Josh took hold of her other hand. 'It was *my* idea that she can make the porridge.'

Cheddar barked again, turning a circle or two before heading towards the pantry, but Isobel wasn't aware of the dog's excitement. The only thing she was aware of was the feeling of those two small hands tugging hers. There seemed to be a direct line between her hands and her heart because she could feel *that* being tugged on too. This was more than simply being charmed by a couple of adorable kids. A whole lot more. Isobel could feel the connection and, as soon as she truly acknowledged it, these boys would be hers. *Her* nephews. Her *family*.

The enormity of the thought was enough to make Isobel freeze and, because Oscar and Josh were still tugging her hands, they lost their grip and turned back in surprise to see what had gone wrong with their plan. Cheddar was also looking back from the door of the pantry, clearly wondering what was taking so long and, for what seemed like a long, long moment, everything stopped—as if the universe was asking Isobel what she was going to do. Take the plunge and invite the twins into her life or take a step back and then flee, like she'd done in the past?

'What on earth is going on in there?' It sounded as if Rafe had only emerged from sleep a few seconds ago. They could all hear the slightly muffled voice coming from the hallway. 'What happened to quiet time until seven o'clock?'

'But Aunty Belle's here, Daddy. She's going to make our porridge,' Josh said.

'She doesn't know about the seven o'clock rule,' Oscar added. 'We only told her about the cleaning up a mess rule.'

Isobel turned her head cautiously as Rafe came into the kitchen, very much hoping he wouldn't be in pyjamas like his sons. He wasn't, but he was still pulling a woollen jersey on and the button on his jeans hadn't been fastened. His hair was rumpled as well and his jaw heavily shadowed.

And, dear Lord…the only thing Isobel could think of was how that overnight stubble used to feel against her skin first thing in the morning…

She looked away instantly. 'I'm sorry if you got woken up,' she said. 'And I do know about the cleaning up rule so I'm about to fix that mess on the table.'

Rafe rubbed his eyes and then moved towards the table. 'Is that instant coffee?' He shook his head. 'I'm guessing you'll be in need of the real stuff this morning. I'll make a pot.' He veered towards the Aga. 'Boys, you can go and get dressed. I'll make your porridge when you come back.'

'But…'

'No "but"s.'

'But, *Daddy*…this "but" is important.'

'Okay.' Rafe put the coffee pot down and crouched, holding his arms out in what looked like a well-rehearsed routine, as one boy nestled within each arm and they both put an arm around Rafe's neck and peered into his face at very close quarters. Isobel had no idea which of the twins was whispering.

'But what if Aunty Belle goes away while we're getting dressed?'

Oh…the anxiety in that question didn't just tug at her heart, it was wrapping itself right round it. There was a new guilt to be found as well. These children were prepared to welcome her into their lives without hesitation and she was suddenly aware of everything she'd missed in the last six years. Those milestones of these babies learning to walk and talk and start school. Rafe looked up to catch her gaze in that instant and she knew that *he* knew exactly what she was thinking. She could guess that he also thought it was no more than she deserved.

'I won't go away, Josh,' she said quietly. 'I promise.'

'I'm Oscar.' The correction was gleeful. 'You got it wrong.'

'Sorry. It might take me a while to make sure I don't get you mixed up.'

'That's okay.' Josh nodded. 'Our grandma used to get it wrong *all* the time.'

'But she's dead now,' Oscar said sadly. 'Like Mummy.'

'And Whistle.' Josh was watching Isobel closely. 'Do you know who Whistle was?'

'No…' Isobel bit her lip. Should she say something about their mother and grandmother? Or go with the flow? 'Um…who *was* Whistle?'

'He was our guinea pig. He whistled. Like—'

'Right…' Rafe's tone was a decisive move to close the conversation. He ruffled the dark curls on both boys' heads. 'Off you go, both of you, and get your school uniforms on.'

The boys went, making odd whistling noises. Isobel bit her lip again but then caught Rafe's gaze and couldn't help a smile emerging, which felt inappropriate given the enormous family loss that had just been mentioned. But Rafe smiled back at her as he straightened and reached for the coffee pot again.

'Never a dull moment round here,' he said. 'And, to be fair, that was a very good imitation of guinea pig noises.'

Isobel watched for a moment as he measured ground coffee beans into the pot and put it on the Aga. A moment later he had a damp dishcloth in his hands and was deftly wiping up the spilt sugar on the table.

'That's my job,' she said. 'I made the mess.'

'I suspect I've had more practice at this than you,' he countered. 'And this is nothing. Sit down. By the time I've fed Cheddar and got the porridge on, that coffee should be about ready.'

Isobel did what she was told and sat down. 'You do it well,' she told Rafe.

'What? Cleaning up?' He'd scooped the last of the granules into the cloth and was heading towards the sink.

She smiled. 'No. I meant the whole "dad" thing.'

That made Rafe pause. He didn't turn around and his voice was quiet but there could be no mistaking his sincerity. 'Those boys,' he said, 'are the best thing that's ever happened to me.'

He held the cloth under the tap to rinse it and then he squeezed it dry and put it down on the bench. It was only then that he turned and looked directly at Isobel.

'That's why I'm prepared to take on raising their half-sister,' he added, even more quietly. 'If no one else that's part of her family can be found to take it on.'

'Meaning me?'

Rafe simply held her gaze for another heartbeat. Then he stooped to pick up a dog bowl and headed for the pantry with Cheddar on his heels.

'The boys are very excited that you're here. I haven't told them that you might want to go to a hotel today.'

Isobel closed her eyes as she took a breath. She could hear the rattle of kibble being poured into the dog bowl. She could smell the coffee that was coming to the boil on the stove. And, if she thought about it, she could still feel the imprint of those small hands tugging on hers only minutes ago. She could also still sense the crossroads she was standing at, where one direction would let her escape but the other would make those little boys a permanent part of her life—and her heart.

Could Rafe sense her hesitation as he came back out of the pantry?

'You did promise that you wouldn't go away.'

He knew as well as she did that she'd only been reassuring the twins that she wouldn't disappear in the time it took them to get dressed but it seemed that he was also offering her a way to say she'd stay longer without them needing to discuss why either of them might not want that. Maybe it was more than that, in fact. This felt as if Rafe was focusing on the future rather than the past. That he was offering her a second chance? A way to make up for at least part of what she'd missed already?

Isobel swallowed hard. 'I won't go away,' she said softly. 'Not yet, anyway. If…you're really okay with that?'

The dog bowl clattered as Cheddar stuck his nose in and moved it across the wooden floor in his enthusiasm to eat his breakfast but Rafe must have heard her tentative query because he gave a single nod.

'I am okay with that,' he said. 'And the boys

will be delighted. This is where you should be. Now, let me get the porridge on and this coffee sorted and then I need to fill you in on what got sorted yesterday with your mother's house. You've got an appointment to meet an insurance assessor later this morning. I'd come with you, but I doubt that I can get away. Our practice nurse got taken to hospital last night with what appears to have been a stroke. Until we can get a replacement, it's going to be a bit chaotic at work.'

'It's not a problem,' Isobel assured him. 'The house is my problem. Thank you very much for getting the ball rolling but I'll take it from here.'

Rafe had arranged for the utilities of water, gas and electricity to be turned off yesterday and he'd contacted Sharon Matthews' solicitor, who'd provided the name of the insurance company.

'You could get a taxi to Barrington Street. Or I could ask Helen to drop you off?'

'It's not that far,' Isobel said. 'A bit of fresh air will be good for me and I should make the most of it not raining. I'll have my car after that. I might drive around and get my bearings again.'

'You could drop into St Luke's if you're in that part of town,' Rafe suggested. 'There are personal things of your mother and Lauren that got collected in ED and it hasn't felt right for me to be the one to pick them up.'

Isobel could understand his reluctance. She found herself thinking that she didn't want to pick them up herself, as she walked towards her mother's house later that morning. Collecting random personal things, like handbags or the last clothes that had been worn, felt like it could well be a lot more challenging than attending the formal ceremony of a funeral. She was still thinking about the funeral when she saw the curtain twitch on the house next door as she stood on the step finding the key and remembered that Louise had been the only person to acknowledge her presence there, other than Rafe. It was no surprise that her mother's friend was coming up the path by the time she had the door open.

'I saw all the comings and goings yesterday,' Louise said. 'And the plumber's van here so I asked him what he was doing. It's awful, isn't it? As if you don't have enough on your plate as it is. I'm very sorry, love.'

'It's not your fault, Louise. It was a burst pipe.'

'But I didn't notice anything wrong and I'm right next door.'

'I'm glad the water didn't get into your house. It's made an awful mess here. I'm afraid there's going to be a bit of disruption for you when they start fixing it.' Isobel looked into the hallway. 'I'm not even going to go inside until the insurance assessor gets here. It's quite dangerous. The whole living room ceiling is on the point of collapsing.'

'Oh, my goodness... Do you want to come and wait at my place? It's a bit warmer inside.'

'I'm okay. The assessor's due here in a few minutes.'

Louise nodded. She opened her mouth and then closed it again, as if she'd thought better of what she intended to say. And then she tried again. 'I never liked it,' she told Isobel. 'I knew that things weren't going so well for you and your boyfriend, but Lauren had no right to jump in like that and steal him. And when I heard she was pregnant, I knew it was no accident. Not that I could say that to Sharon.

Not without ruining our friendship. I didn't blame you, though…for not talking to either of them after that.'

'I don't think boyfriends get stolen unless they want to be,' Isobel said evasively. She really didn't want to get into a blame apportioning discussion. 'But we can't change the past.'

'Aye…true enough. And the future's a mystery. Goodness me, who would have thought that this would happen?'

'Mmm…' Isobel tilted her head to look up the street. Was the insurance assessor running late?

'Your mum was planning to sell this place,' Louise said. 'She was going to go and live in Spain with Lauren. She was right miffed when Lauren said she was coming back here to have her baby. It was the first Sharon knew that she was even pregnant again.'

'Oh?' Isobel wasn't sure she wanted to discuss this with Louise either.

'Well, we all knew she hadn't been able to handle motherhood the first time round with the twins, so why on earth was she doing it again? Your mother didn't enjoy helping with the twins either. Said she "couldn't be bothered with babies at her stage in life".'

Isobel was watching someone park a car further up the street but she was thinking about the twins. About how adorable they were. About that picture of them she'd carried in her wallet for so long. How could anyone have not wanted to 'be bothered'? Rafe had been bothered. He'd said that the twins were the best thing that had ever happened to him. And the palpable bond between them had been striking. The way they'd wrapped their arms around their dad's neck to discuss the important 'but'. Did her mother ever think about what she might have been missing out on?

'Why didn't Mum want to have anything to do with her grandsons?' she asked Louise. 'After Lauren had left?'

Louise seemed to be watching the man who was now getting out of his car. He had a clipboard in his hands.

'It was all very awkward. And Sharon really couldn't cope with trying to help with two babies at the same time. And then they got old enough to talk and would ask her when their mummy was coming back or if she still loved them and that made her feel guilty, I suppose. She saw them sometimes. For their birthdays.

She usually went to Spain for Christmas. She loved the sunshine in winter.'

'She would have known Lauren's partner, then? The baby's father?'

'Oh, no...' Louise made a tutting sound. 'I don't think even Lauren knew who that was. Or, if she did, she never told her mother. She worked as a barmaid and loved living the high life. There was a new boyfriend every few weeks as far as I heard.'

She got bored...and then she needed to find something else...

But her sister had decided to keep her baby. Had she finally realised how lonely her lifestyle was? Had she wanted to come back to England to be part of a family? To be with her sons again, even?

'Hi. Are you Isobel?' The man had reached the gate.

'Yes.'

'I'm Colin. From Sure Shield Insurance? I'm here to assess the damage from the flooding.'

'I'd better leave you to it.' Louise patted Isobel's arm. 'Just knock if you want a chat any time, dear. I'm always at home.'

And probably lonely. She was going to miss

having her friend next door. Isobel smiled at the older woman. 'I'll let you know what's happening with the house as soon as I know myself.'

With the first shock of having seen the damage in her mother's house over, Isobel found she was noticing far more personal items today as she went through with Colin, the insurance assessor, and her reaction only confirmed that it might be confronting to go and collect those personal items from the hospital.

Just seeing a pair of reading glasses and a novel on a cluttered bedside table brought a wave of sadness that was unbelievably deep. Her mum had loved getting lost in a romantic fantasy. The small photograph beside the lamp, of her mother and Lauren, looked like it had been taken in Spain and it hammered home how little Isobel had known of their lives in recent years. Had this been taken at Christmastime? She could imagine them both having such a good time, eating tapas and flirting outrageously with any man willing to play. Had she been more jealous than she'd ever admitted of the close relationship her sister had had with their mother? And could that have been as damaging to the fabric of family as Lauren's jealousy of everything Isobel had had in her life? Like her career? Like Rafe?

She could throw some confusion in with the guilt and grief now. She turned away from the photograph to follow the assessor out of the room

'Not so bad up here,' he was saying. 'The main damage is downstairs, of course. Bit of mould happening, though. Nasty stuff. It'll all have to be thrown out. Carpets, wallpaper, curtains. Probably the mattresses in these bedrooms as well.'

Isobel followed him into the smaller upstairs bedrooms that had been hers and Lauren's. Her old room was completely bare of any childhood memories but there was a shelf in Lauren's that held a few old toys, including a small, soft hand-knitted teddy bear that had originally been Isobel's. A slightly misshaped bear that had oddly short limbs and one ear much larger than the other, but Lauren had wanted it and Isobel, at about the age that Josh and Oscar were now, had only hesitated for a heartbeat before giving it to the baby sister she'd adored. Without thinking, grownup Isobel took the bear from the shelf and tucked it into her shoulder bag as she followed the assessor downstairs.

'I've done a few of these jobs,' he told her. 'There's a process to go through. First up, we'll get the rest of the water pumped out and then one of our specialist cleaning contractors will come through. Everything water-damaged will get thrown out and they can clear anything else you don't want. This is an estate clearance as well, yes? You're planning to sell the place?'

'Yes.'

'You'll need to come and get anything you want to keep before the cleaners get started then.'

'Okay.'

'The next step is stripping the house—downstairs, for sure and the bathroom upstairs. The floorboards will have to be replaced—maybe the subfloor as well. The wall coverings have to come off too, so that the studs get a chance to dry out, otherwise you'll end up having big problems down the track. And that living room ceiling's got to go pronto, if it hasn't fallen down by itself before the builders get in.'

'How long is it going to take?'

'Weeks. Especially at this time of year. You can't leave damp anywhere because it's just a health hazard. Nobody would want to buy the house if it's not done properly. And drying it out is just the start. After that, it has to get re-built and that can take even longer, depending on how busy our building contractors happen to be. Sorry, it's not going to be a quick fix. This is going to take months.'

Isobel was thinking about the complications this was going to cause. She'd taken a single month's leave from her job in New Zealand, thinking that would be more than enough time to clean out the house and put it on the market, but it felt as if the walls of a trap were closing around her now. How could she leave before things were sorted here? But how could she stay for that long? Even Rafe, with his firm ideals about supporting an extended family member, would be justifiably daunted by that prospect but she couldn't afford a hotel on top of keeping up the rent on her apartment in New Zealand.

'At least it's covered by the insurance,' the assessor said. 'It would cost a fortune otherwise. I'll keep you posted, yes? Might be best to leave it a few days before coming to get what you want out of the place.'

Isobel could feel the lump of the teddy bear in her bag under her arm. 'I don't think I want anything,' she said quietly. 'It might be better if the cleaning company just sorts it out.'

The assessor gave her a curious glance. 'I'll get in touch anyway. You might change your mind.'

Isobel did change her mind once she was in her rental car and turning onto one of Balclutha's main roads. Not about searching the house for keepsakes but about picking up her mother's and sister's Patient's Property bags from St Luke's Hospital. She decided she might as well get the worst things out of the way on the same day. It wasn't as if she had to open the bags straight away, after all.

The route to the hospital was easy to remember and brought other memories along with it. How excited had she been, after graduating from her nursing degree to get a job at Balclutha's most prestigious hospital? And then to end up working in the emergency department, which was a dream come true, especially after she'd moved into her own tiny apartment in the nurses' accommodation block near the hospital.

Lauren had been so envious of her independence, although not enough to move away from being waited on hand and foot by a doting mother. She'd envied the exciting job Isobel had too, but her attempt to follow her sister's career choice became unstuck when she failed her first set of Health Science exams at university. She'd never been able to stand the sight of blood anyway. Becoming a receptionist at the hospital's main entrance had been a much better fit for someone who was happy to talk to anyone and could charm them all.

They'd been so very different, but Isobel had truly loved her sister and made allowances for any shortcomings. Until that last, unforgivable incident. She'd never intended the estrangement to become permanent, however. She'd gone away for Christmas that year and then arranged a transfer to a London hospital, a few hours' drive away. It was the news that Lauren was pregnant that rubbed salt into an unhealed wound. And then, much later, after the twins had been born, that wedding invitation had been enough to send her as far

away as she could get—without leaving a for-
warding address.

But the blame couldn't be laid purely on
one side of the equation, could it? Lauren had
been at least partially justified in her denial
that she'd broken up Isobel and Rafe's relationship because they'd broken up weeks ago,
hadn't they? Maybe she'd also been correct in
suggesting that it was just wishful thinking
on Isobel's part that Rafe was going to realise
how much he was missing her and change his
mind about the breakup. She needed to get
over it and move on, her mother had chipped
in. All Lauren had done was to help her see
that Rafe wasn't the man for her.

And, while Isobel might have done what
she felt she had to do to protect herself at the
time, had she gone too far, for too long? The
love that had once been there for her mother
and her sister hadn't disappeared, it had just
been buried beneath layers of hurt and anger.
The finality of knowing she could never do
anything to even try to put things right was
making the waves of grief unbearable and Isobel found herself in the hospital car park, with
her head resting on her hands on the steering
wheel, sobbing uncontrollably for a long time.

No wonder Rafe was less than impressed with her, she decided, when emotional exhaustion began muting any grief and her tears finally began to dry up. She didn't much like the person she seemed to have become herself. Things had always seemed so black and white, and she'd considered herself to have been the only one who'd been betrayed, but it wasn't really that simple, was it? Rafe had been betrayed by his ex-wife before his time with Isobel and he'd made it very clear he wasn't looking for a permanent, committed relationship with her but she hadn't been able to keep hiding how much in love with him she was so it shouldn't have come as a shock that he'd backed off.

He'd been betrayed again when Lauren had walked out with another man, from not only their marriage but her own children. He'd done the 'right thing' all along though, hadn't he? He'd ended the relationship as gently as possible with the woman who'd wanted more than he was able to give. He'd married the woman who'd accidentally become pregnant by him. He was raising his sons alone—and doing a damn good job of that, from what Isobel had seen. He was even prepared to raise the boys' half-sister.

A baby who was here—in this hospital's Neonatal Intensive Care Unit—without any family around her. Without even a name.

Isobel wiped the last tears from her face and gathered her coat and bag to get out of the car. A new thought was gaining traction in both her head and her heart. Maybe it wasn't too late to try and put something right, after all. As she reached the main entrance of the hospital it almost felt as if Rafe was watching her and Isobel knew he would approve of what she was planning to do. There was a tiny gleam of warmth to be found there. Not because it had once been so important to win his approval. This was more to do with how Isobel felt about herself. About her own need to do the 'right thing'.

Because she'd changed her mind again. She wasn't going to go and find the bags of personal property that would be in safe keeping somewhere in the basement of St Luke's. She was going to go to the NICU.

To meet her niece.

CHAPTER FOUR

Baby Tanner

THAT WAS THE name above the incubator Isobel was led to in the NICU, having introduced herself to the staff on duty.

'You're her aunt? Oh…that's fabulous.' They had welcomed her appearance. 'We were starting to wonder if we'd ever discover a family member for our wee Button.'

'Not that Dr Tanner hasn't been amazing,' another nurse put in. 'But it's a big ask for him to take centre stage. Nobody's been able to track down even a hint of who the father might be and we knew that you were the only relative on Mum's side. We weren't sure you even knew about the birth, though.'

'I didn't,' Isobel admitted. 'Not until yesterday.'

'You're here now, that's what matters. Let's

get you a gown and mask and some hand sanitiser and you can come and meet your niece. She's a little miracle as far as we're concerned—the only baby we've ever had who's been born after...'

Her voice trailed away and Isobel could feel the wave of sympathy from everyone in this central desk area of the Neonatal Intensive Care Unit.

'We're so sorry for your loss,' someone said quietly.

A pager bleeped and one of the doctors moved away swiftly. A nurse responded to the quiet but insistent sound of a nearby monitoring alarm going off and a parent came to ask for assistance from another staff member. It was an older nurse, Brenda, who took Isobel to one of the closest positions to the central desk, where Baby Tanner's incubator was in direct sight at all times.

'We all try to spend as much time as possible with her,' Brenda said, 'but it gets too busy so she still has too much time alone. She's touched everyone's hearts here, that's for sure.'

Isobel nodded, her gaze fixed on the tiny baby in front of her. There were heart-shaped patches sticking heart monitoring electrodes in place, nasal cannula taped to her face delivering oxygen and IV lines under bandages. The baby seemed to be awake and, distressingly, seemed to be less than happy. A tiny hand waved in the air, sticklike little legs were trying to kick and her mouth was open although no sound was being made. The squeeze in Isobel's chest made it hard to take a breath.

'She's not in pain, is she?' Isobel asked.

Brenda was checking all the screens surrounding the incubator. 'I don't think so. Nothing's changed in the last hour and if she was in pain I'd expect her heart rate and blood pressure to have gone up. We have all been too rushed to have anyone sitting with her for a while though. Maybe she's lonely, which means you've timed your visit perfectly.' She smiled at Isobel and gestured towards the comfortable recliner chair that was beside the incubator. 'Take a seat. I'll have a word with her consultant and see if it's okay for her to come out of the incubator for you to hold her for a bit.'

Someone was pushing a trolley past them. 'Brenda, have you got a minute? I could do with some help.'

'Will you be okay?' Brenda asked. 'I'll come back as soon as I can,' she added as Isobel nodded. 'In the meantime, you can put your hand through one of the holes and hold hers, if you like.'

Isobel sank onto the edge of the chair. She hadn't expected to be allowed anything more than a peep at this fragile newborn baby and to perhaps be allowed to leave the little teddy bear she had in her bag somewhere nearby, if not at the foot of the incubator's mattress. She certainly wouldn't have asked to touch the baby, let alone hold her, and she hesitated now, even though she'd been given permission. Maybe part of her knew that touching this infant would make it all more real somehow. That she would be stepping forward to play her part in this tiny human's future. To take responsibility even?

After the emotional release of her heartbroken crying in the car, Isobel was too drained to think about something so huge and maybe, if it hadn't looked as if the baby was trying, and failing, to cry, Isobel might have resisted the urge to touch her for more than a minute or two. But, with everyone so busy around her, it felt as if she was the only one who could offer comfort. More than that, she wanted to be able to comfort this baby who had, as far as anyone could ever know, been born an orphan.

Isobel put her hand in through the access port, reaching out gently with a single fingertip to touch the miniature hand lying palm up on the mattress. Almost instantly, those impossibly tiny fingers closed and Isobel could feel the warmth and a surprising strength in the grip. What was even more surprising and just as instantaneous was the feeling that it wasn't just her finger being held. Her heart was also well and truly caught.

This was more than the invitation to be part of their lives that the twins had unknowingly given her this morning when they'd been tugging on her hands. This was…just there. And this wasn't going to be a case of choosing whether or not she took responsibility for this baby, because that was just there as well. The logistics might prove to be complicated and overturn her life completely but there was no way Isobel could walk away from this—something that the grip of those tiny fingers was telling her was the most important thing that had ever happened in her life.

When the neonatal specialist came to talk to her a short time later, Isobel had only one urgent question about the care of her niece.

'What can I do to help?'

Rafe Tanner checked his watch as he left the cardiology ward and then took the stairs up instead of down. If he was quick, he could pop in to see the baby before heading home at the end of an overly busy day.

Seeing the screens around the incubator was alarming because that usually meant some kind of potentially serious intervention was going on but, as he paused to rub sanitiser gel onto his hands, he caught the eye of a nurse who was busy with another baby and was reassured. Brenda's smile, in fact, suggested that things were better than simply good. She even gave him a quick 'thumbs up' signal.

And what he found behind the screens a moment later was nothing like he had expected. There were no medical staff in this space and no procedures happening. There was also no baby in the incubator. There was, however, someone sitting in the reclining chair with her feet up, a blanket draped around her body and a look on her face that made Rafe catch his breath.

'I'm doing kangaroo care,' Isobel whispered.

Wow...

Just...wow...

Rafe couldn't say anything yet. He moved to the side of the big chair and crouched down, resting his elbows on its padded arms, and then he stayed there, completely still for the longest time, just getting his head around so many unexpected things.

Isobel was wearing a hospital gown, opened at the front, and the baby was nestled between her breasts, on her bare skin, the soft blanket covering them both for warmth. It was the first time Rafe had seen this tiny baby out of the incubator and she seemed smaller but somehow less fragile. She was asleep and the soft, steady beeping of the monitors was evidence that her heart and respiration rates, blood pressure and the oxygen saturation in her blood were well within desired parameters. Even without any of that technology, however, Rafe would have known that this baby was calm and contented.

So was Isobel. Perhaps it was because she

was wearing a mask that her eyes seemed so much more expressive. Or maybe it was what he was seeing in them. Catching and holding her gaze over the tiny head in its little woollen hat, he could almost feel the connection she had found with the baby and it reminded him of the kind of overwhelming feelings he'd had when he'd held his newborn twins for the first time.

It also reminded him of the way he'd begun to feel within such a short time of becoming very close to Isobel Matthews. When he'd begun to wonder how sure he really was that he could never truly trust another woman. Or that there was no such thing as love at first sight...

It had been a new kind of love in his life when the boys arrived, however. One that gave him so much joy and kept him busy enough that he could ignore any disturbing reminders that he might be missing out on something else that was just as important. The thing he'd lost when Isobel walked out of his life?

It was Isobel who finally broke that eye contact and it felt as if she'd been reluctant to do so. Her breath hitched as she drew it in.

'I asked what I could to help,' she said softly. 'And the doctor told me that this was the best thing I could do. It can stabilise heart rate and breathing and improve oxygen saturation. Research is suggesting that it can even have a positive effect on brain development that shows up when they're older.'

Rafe nodded. 'I've read about it. It didn't occur to me to offer though. I guess I thought it was too early for her to be held yet.'

'I'm just doing it for an hour today, but it can be more than that. I could do several hours a day by next week, if she's well. And if I want to.'

Rafe swallowed what felt like a lump in his throat. 'Do you? Want to?'

Isobel was looking down at the baby's head and she was blinking rapidly as if trying to prevent tears gathering but she was nodding at the same time. 'Looks like I'm stuck here for a while. The insurance assessor told me it will take weeks to even dry out the house before any repair work can start.'

'Oh...'

Rafe watched the exquisite gentleness with which Isobel was cupping the baby's head with her hand and he could feel an odd sensation in his gut, as if a knot the same size as that head was forming—and being held. He wasn't sure whether it was a pleasant sensation or something to be concerned about. A warning, even? When Isobel glanced up, he could see a question in her eyes as well and he realised that this was new ground for both of them.

Maybe it could be a completely new start?

'That's good,' he added. 'I mean, it will be wonderful for this little one.' He dropped his gaze to the baby. 'And it will be great for Oscar and Josh.' Again, he had to swallow hard. He didn't know what to say about how he felt about it himself and he suspected that Isobel had the same kind of internal conflict going on. But he needed to say something. 'It's good,' he repeated. 'It's…good to see you again, Belle.'

And it was, now that the first shock had worn off. It would be good to be able to put the past behind them, if that was possible. To forgive, if not exactly forget.

She didn't look up. They were both keeping their gazes firmly on the baby and Isobel said nothing for a long moment. Then she cleared her throat quietly.

'I've thought of a name,' she said.

'What's that?'

The baby moved her head when Isobel lifted her hand. Her tiny arm stretched out towards Rafe and he touched her hand as he'd done many times through the access port on the incubator. As always, her tiny fingers curled around his and gave him that over-powering wave of connection. Maybe it was because she was lying on Isobel's skin that made it feel as if the connection was travel-ling via that tiny body to include Isobel as well. She was always going to be a part of his life, wasn't she?

'She's so small and delicate,' Isobel said. 'It made me think of holding a flower and being careful not to bruise a petal or stem. And my favourite flower has always been a daisy. What do you think? Could we call her Daisy?'

What did he think?

He could see that Isobel was smiling behind her mask by the way those crinkles appeared by her eyes. His first thought, however, was a memory of a picnic on a lazy late-summer Sunday afternoon when he was lying on a grassy hill with her. When he was becoming aware that he was falling in love with her but hadn't defined what that feeling was. In that delicious space of time before the alarm bells began ringing loudly enough to be impossible to ignore. He'd idly started picking daisies from the grass that day, making a chain to rest on Isobel's sunshine-coloured curls:

'Daisies are absolutely my favourite flowers. I love them so much...'

Her eyes had told him that she loved him even more than daisies and the sun had been shining and, for just a few wonderful minutes, he'd never been so happy in his life. He'd kissed her. So slowly it had made time stand still. And when the world had started turning again, before he remembered what it was like to have your heart broken and convinced himself that he had to get away before it could happen to him again, he'd kissed her a second time, even more slowly...

His voice was raw when he found some words.

'I think that's a great name.'

Oscar and Josh also thought it was a great name when Rafe told them as they were eating dinner that evening.

'She's our sister, isn't she?'

'Half-sister.'

'What's a half-sister?'

'It means that Daisy has the same mummy but a different daddy.'

'Why aren't *you* her daddy? You're our daddy.'

Isobel caught the long blink that suggested Rafe was finding this line of questioning from his sons difficult.

'Because Mummy hasn't lived with us for a long, long time. So I couldn't be Daisy's daddy, could I?'

Surprisingly, it didn't seem to cause the children any distress to be reminded that their mother had abandoned them years ago. It was simply a fact of life. Was that because it had happened when they were so young they had no memories of Lauren? While it was an acceptable answer, however, it wasn't the end of the questions.

'Where's she going to sleep?'

'She has to stay in the hospital for a while, Josh. She was born too early so she's very, very little.'

'But when she comes home, where's she going to sleep?'

'She can be in our room,' Oscar suggested.

'That's very kind,' Rafe said. 'But I think

your room is quite full with both you boys in it and all those toys.'

'She can be in Aunty Belle's room then.'

Was Rafe deliberately avoiding catching Isobel's gaze?

'Eat your beans up,' he said. 'Green things are good for you.'

'I don't like beans.'

'I don't like anything green.' Josh was backing his brother up. 'Do you like green things, Aunty Belle?'

'Green things are my favourite,' she told them. This was good. They had moved away from the subject of where Daisy was going to sleep, which was too big to even think about today. Especially now, only hours after she'd had that tiny baby sleeping right on top of her heart—and when jetlag was hitting all over again and Isobel knew she would probably need to go to bed at the same time these six-year-old boys did.

'Beans, broccoli, spinach,' she added. 'They're all my favourites.' She picked up a bean with her fingers and ate it with a smile to demonstrate how much she liked green things. The boys shared an open-mouthed glance and then grinned at their father.

'Aunty Belle didn't use her fork.'

'Mmm…' Rafe seemed just as relieved that the subject had been changed. 'I guess she knows that eating beans is more important than the way you put them in your mouth.'

The twins shared another glance and grin. And then they both picked up a bean with their fingers and ate it. Rafe shared a glance with Isobel and the corner of his mouth twitched as he suppressed a smile.

'When you've finished your beans, you can have half an hour of television while I clean up and then I'm going to hear your reading homework, okay?'

'Can't Aunty Belle hear our reading homework?'

'Not tonight,' Rafe said firmly. 'She's tired, aren't you, Belle?'

Had he been aware of how much effort it had been to stay awake enough to eat the delicious dinner that Helen the housekeeper had left keeping warm in the Aga? Or was he hoping she'd go to her room early so that he could relax with his sons like any normal evening?

She wasn't about to rush off, however, because she'd remembered something she should probably have told Rafe earlier, but she needed to wait until two small boys were out of earshot.

'I spoke to Mum's neighbour today, when I was at the house,' she told him as she carried plates to where he was stacking the dishwasher. 'They've been friends ever since I was a kid and told each other everything. She said that Lauren never said anything about Daisy's father. That she might not have actually known who it was herself.'

The implication that there could be a choice of men in his ex-wife's life didn't seem to surprise Rafe.

'Yeah… The police made some enquiries at the bar where Lauren was working. Nobody could remember who she was with around the time she would have become pregnant and there were more than a few one-night stands.' He was bent over, fitting cutlery into the tray on the bottom shelf of the dishwasher. 'I guess she never found what she was looking for, which is kind of a sad way to go through life, isn't it?'

He straightened and took a plate from Isobel's hands.

'I would never have chosen to marry Lauren,' he said quietly. 'I was being completely honest with you when I said I never wanted to get married again. Or have kids. But she told me that if I didn't marry her, I'd never see the twins. That my name wouldn't even be on the birth certificate. I grew up without a father in my own life. My mother told me he was dead but when I was about ten I found out she'd lied to me—he just hadn't wanted me.' Rafe put the plate in the rack and then met Isobel's gaze as he reached for another one. 'I've never forgotten that first taste of feeling rejected. Betrayed, even, and the thought of that happening to my own children was unacceptable. It was just after they were born. Just after I'd held them for the first time...'

Oh... Isobel knew what that was like. How a newborn baby could capture you, heart and soul, with a connection that would be there until you took your last breath. Daisy had done that to her today and she wasn't even this infant's mother. Imagine how much more powerful it could be if it was your own children, even if you'd believed you never wanted them? How you could not fall instantly in love and be prepared to do whatever it took not to lose them?

Rafe was holding the plate in her hands

now, but Isobel hadn't let go of it. It almost
felt as if Rafe was holding her hands—the
way he was also holding her gaze.

'I never wanted to marry your sister.' The
words were no more than a murmur. 'You
were the one I loved, Belle.'

CHAPTER FIVE

WORDS.

That was all they were.

Only a very few of them, in fact, so how was it that they could have the effect of a bomb going off in your life?

We need to stop seeing each other...

You slept with my sister...

She's pregnant. It's twins...

You were the one I loved, Belle...

They'd never actually used the 'L' word in the time they'd been together but Isobel had been convinced it had been hanging in the air between them for days. Ever since that gorgeous picnic on the hill when he'd crowned her with a daisy chain. She had to wait for Rafe to say it first, though. And even then she'd known she would have to give him all the time and space he needed to be able to trust the idea of a future together. To change his mind, even, about the commitment that marriage could bestow? She'd been happy to wait. She'd wanted to be sure it was safe, herself, before opening that portal to a future that was glowing with the potential for life to be everything she could have dreamed of.

Would it have made a difference if Isobel had managed to get to that fateful Christmas party and had said something to Rafe that night? If she'd told him how desperately she was missing him? That he was the person she wanted to be with for the rest of her life?

Would it make a difference now?

Yes.

Isobel's body clearly thought so as she lay, sleepless, in her bed later that night, aware of the tingling sensation that was coming from somewhere in her gut and spreading into her limbs—almost like the first hint of the 'pins and needles' that signalled a compressed nerve starting to function again to bring a foot or hand back to life—only this was surely far more emotional than physical. Was it excitement coming back to life?

Hope…?

How she'd escaped the kitchen without responding to Rafe's extraordinary confession was a bit of a blur but she could remember jetlag being mentioned despite her head spinning so much she couldn't think straight. The twins' competition to be first for a goodnight cuddle was easy to remember too, because it had almost knocked her off her feet, made Cheddar bark with loud approval of this new game and earned a reprimand for everyone from Rafe.

The house was quiet now. She could imagine Cheddar asleep on the old couch in the kitchen. Perhaps the twins were also asleep, or was Rafe in their bedroom reading them a story with a son snuggled in on each side of his body? She could imagine peeping through a bedroom door to see that as well. Maybe some of that tingling had reached her brain now as well, because it was more than willing to run with that image and let her imagine that she was the mother of those children. That Rafe would finish the story, tuck sleepy boys into their beds and then come to find *her*. It then deftly skipped the mundane part of any evening parental chores that might have needed doing after that and got straight to the part where he took her to *their* bed.

It wasn't even fantasy after that. There were

buried but unforgotten memories of exactly what it had been like to be in Raphael Tanner's bed. How he could look at you as if no other woman had ever existed. How he could touch—and taste—your skin as if it was the most delicate and delicious thing ever created. How he could take you to the brink of ecstasy and just hold you there to build the anticipation to a point where the climax took you to a place where time and location had no meaning. All that there was in that timeless space was how close you were to this man you loved so much.

How perfect it felt…

Oh, *help*… Isobel rolled onto her side, seeking a softer patch on her pillow and hoping that her brain might realise how badly her body needed sleep and switch off so that it could happen some time very soon.

Why had he said that?

Did he still have feelings for her?

Did she *want* him to still have feelings for her?

Yes.

No.

He'd betrayed her. With her *sister*. It would have been quite bad enough knowing that he'd made love to any other woman but for it to have been Lauren…well, there was no coming back from that because it had touched something so deep it felt as if it had been there for ever. Lauren had always been the favourite. More special because she had been born after their father had died. So much prettier with her platinum shade of shiny, straight blonde hair rather than the messy, dark gold riot of curls that Isobel had and eyes that were a much paler shade of blue. That smile could get her anything she wanted and that ability to capture and hold the attention of those around her and simply…bring joy, that was what it had been. Isobel had loved her butterfly of a sister as much as anyone, until she'd taken something she knew she would never be able to find again.

The ability to believe that she wasn't second best. That the man she'd fallen so completely and utterly in love with had wanted to be with her because *she* was the special one. Because he loved *her*. And she'd known he had loved her. She'd seen it in his eyes when he'd put that crown of daisies on her head. Just before he'd kissed her senseless. And, okay, he'd backed off but she'd been so sure that he was missing her as much as she was missing him. He'd looked so miserable at work, despite the anticipation of Christmas festivities. When he'd asked if she was going to the party, she'd been sure that there was every chance they would be together again by the end of the evening.

Now she knew that Rafe had never been in love with Lauren. He wouldn't have chosen to marry her if he hadn't been blackmailed. That the marriage to protect his right to be a father to his newborn children had only lasted a matter of months.

That *she* was the woman he'd loved.

And a part of Isobel knew—a big part that was currently the obstacle to her falling asleep—that everything was shifting. Changing. Puzzle pieces had been thrown into the air and she could see them floating.

Maybe it was a combination of jetlag and the trauma of major loss in her life. Or perhaps it was a form of procrastination because she wasn't ready to seriously consider the daunting responsibility she would be taking on if she stepped up to raise Daisy. It could even be that this was a process of finally dealing with things she had avoided confronting for far too long, like the complex family dynamics she had grown up with but, whatever the emotional alchemy that was going on, Isobel could see the possibility that, if she allowed it to happen, those puzzle pieces could settle and form an image that might be eerily similar to the future she'd dreamed about long ago.

He shouldn't have said that.

Things were already complicated enough without dredging up something from the past that was best left buried. How much more awkward was it going to be to have Isobel in his house now?

At least she seemed to be sleeping later this morning and Rafe avoided any awkwardness by leaving the house the moment Helen arrived to look after the boys and get them to school. He was well on the way to Harrison Street Medical Centre by the time he realised he'd left his phone on the kitchen bench but he didn't turn around. The phone had been on the bench because he'd received a text to let him know that the temporary practice nurse who'd worked with them yesterday was not coming back for a second day and, unless the agency could find someone else in a hurry, it meant they would all be under enough extra pressure to make things potentially chaotic. Even a small head start on his working day was too valuable to sacrifice.

It should have also meant that Rafe would have no head space to consider that ill-advised confession he'd made to Isobel when they'd been clearing the table last night. As soon as he stepped into his consulting room, he got on with the urgent admin tasks that were already piling up. There were blood and pathology test results coming in, discharge summaries and specialists' reports to read and prescriptions to sign that would be being collected from reception as soon as the doors opened at nine o'clock for morning surgeries. He only had half an hour before he needed to take telephone triage for calls requesting same-day appointments so this was quite likely to be the least stressful time of his day. Perhaps that was why errant thoughts were able to sneak into the back of his mind in between his focus on a report or when he was waiting for the printer to spit out a new batch of prescriptions to sign.

He really shouldn't have told Isobel that

he'd loved her but not her sister. He *wouldn't* have said it, if he hadn't been on what felt like an uncontrollable emotional rollercoaster ever since he'd seen her with that tiny premature baby nestled between her breasts. The baby she'd chosen to call Daisy. And the kind of expression on her face that he knew meant that she was in love.

The way she had once been in love with him...

He'd known that, even if she hadn't said anything, by the way she'd looked at him. By the way she'd touched him. But it had been vital for it to remain unspoken because he'd needed to be able to trust it. To let his own barriers down enough to not only accept that he felt the same way but to find the courage to take the risk of a commitment that could shape the rest of his life.

It would have been a daunting prospect for any man, let alone someone who'd already done it once only to have been betrayed in such a devastating fashion. That blow had come completely out of left field many years ago now. His wife had not only been having an affair with a colleague for the entirety of their marriage, she was leaving him because the baby she was carrying was not his.

He had found that courage, though. Just pushing Isobel away had been enough to make him realise how much he did want her in his life and he'd been going to tell her that at the Christmas party.

Did Lauren telling him that he was too late—that Belle had already moved on to a colleague—excuse what had happened after that?

No. Of course it didn't.

He hadn't blamed Isobel for hating him for what had happened but he had largely managed to bury it, the way he'd chosen to leave behind the total failure of both his marriages. It was hardly surprising that the shocking events of the last few weeks, with the tragic accident, Daisy's birth, the funeral and seeing Isobel again was stirring up everything he'd thought he'd left behind.

What Rafe wanted, more than anything else right now, was to simply go back to what had become his life as a hard-working GP and a devoted dad to his two boys. He could at least try to make that happen for the next several hours, as he focused on the patients who needed his help.

Like Susan Sugden, the young mother who was on the other end of the first telephone triage call he picked up. He could hear her productive cough over the phone and her symptoms, that included uncontrollable shivering and an episode of coughing up blood, sounded worrying.

'It sounds like this has become more than just the cold that's going around,' he told her. 'Can you come into the surgery or do you need a home visit?'

'I can come in. I've got to get the older kids to school, anyway, so it's on my way home.' Susan sounded exhausted. 'Mum's got her yoga class this morning so she's not helping with the school run today.'

By the time Susan arrived for her urgent appointment, it was clear that the potential for chaos had become reality. It was only half past nine but every chair in the waiting room was occupied and there was a small queue waiting for the attention of their receptionist. Rafe's colleagues were all busy with consultations already and Susan was looking pale and unwell enough for alarm bells to ring. On top of that, the toddler in the stroller she was pushing had flushed cheeks and a runny nose and could well end up being an unexpected extra patient. This wasn't the time to think about the inevitable tension that would ramp up with increased waiting times for everyone else, however.

'Come this way, Susan. And…is it Dylan?'

'Yes. He's got this horrible cold as well… It's been through…the whole family now… I just can't seem to shake it…'

His patient's broken sentences were an indication of how short of breath she was and Rafe's rapid assessment of other vital signs had him heading back to the reception desk only minutes later. The queue had been dealt with but there was another person coming through the door. Rafe stepped close enough to keep his conversation with the receptionist as private as possible.

'Deb, could you please call for an ambulance? I need to send Susan Sugden through to hospital. Get hold of her mum too—the number will be her emergency contact on her file. We'll need her to come and look after Dylan.'

'Sure.' As Rafe turned away Deb was open-

ing a window on her computer that would
give her the information she needed. 'I'll be
with you in just a moment,' he heard her say
to the new arrival.

'No problem. I just need to leave this for
Dr Tanner.'

Rafe swung back. 'Isobel...what on earth
are you doing here?'

'You forgot your phone.' She held it out. 'I
thought you might need it.'

'Thanks...' He reached out to take it. This
was disconcerting enough to add a new level
to the tension in this crowded space. There
was a baby howling in its mother's arms, an
elderly gentleman talking very loudly on his
phone, a pre-school child throwing toys out
of the playpen in the corner and someone
holding a plastic bag in front of their face
as though they were about to be sick. Isobel
didn't seem fazed by the chaos but her eyes
did widen as someone rushed towards the reception desk from the direction of the consulting rooms, her baby in her arms.

'Dr Tanner? It's Dylan...he woke up coughing and...and now he can't breathe...'

The toddler was in Isobel's arms by the
time Rafe got to the other side of the desk.

He could hear the harsh sounds of stridor and wheezing which were warning signs that an airway was getting dangerously obstructed. He could also see the way Isobel was holding the child upright in a cuddle and calming him by her soothing tone and he was instantly reminded of how good she'd been with paediatric patients in the emergency department when they'd worked together. Always calm and capable and caring and the kids had seemed to recognise that. She'd been the nurse everyone wanted for their youngest patients.

'Hey, Dylan…let's get you feeling better, sweetheart…' She looked up as Rafe got closer. 'Where's your treatment room?'

'This way…' Rafe didn't try and take Dylan from her arms. Creating any more anxiety would only add to his respiratory distress and could potentially turn a serious situation into a life-or-death emergency.

'Is there any chance of this being a foreign body obstruction?'

'No.' Rafe followed Isobel into the treatment room, a hand on Susan's arm to support her. 'He's been asleep in his stroller while I was checking his mum.' He guided Susan to the chair at the end of the examination couch. 'Try and focus on your own breathing right now,' he told her. 'And let us do our job and look after Dylan.'

Isobel started to put Dylan onto the bed, but he clung to her neck.

'Stay like that,' Rafe said. 'I'll listen to his chest first and then we'll try and get some oxygen on.'

Isobel was looking over Dylan's shoulder at his mother. 'Tripod position,' she murmured.

He nodded, fitting his stethoscope into his ears. He knew that Susan was demonstrating a classic indication of respiratory distress by leaning forward as she sat, propping herself up with her hands on her knees.

'Bilateral pneumonia,' he told her. 'The whole family's been sick with a respiratory virus so it's likely to be a secondary infection. She's got haemoptysis, tachypnoea and tachycardia. Fever and rigors. I've got an ambulance on the way to take her into hospital, but we should get some oxygen on her as well.'

We. It felt oddly normal to be working with Isobel, even if she wasn't in any kind of uniform. It was also reassuring. Judging by the way she'd dealt with the cardiac arrest at the funeral, she hadn't lost any of her medical skills.

'Dylan's running a temperature too,' she said now. 'And I can feel the respiratory effort he's making.'

'I knew he was looking flushed.' Rafe was silent for a moment as he listened to the amplified chest sounds of a small body struggling to breathe well. 'I was going to check him as soon as we'd made the arrangements to get Susan looked after.'

'Croup?' Isobel suggested quietly. 'Bronchiolitis? Epiglottitis?' She was still rocking Dylan gently.

Epiglottitis was the most serious diagnosis to consider here and it was definitely a possibility, given that it could be caused by the same bacteria that could cause the pneumonia that Dylan's mother had. It was also a condition that could rapidly deteriorate and cause a respiratory arrest that might need a major intervention like an emergency cricothyroidotomy to open an airway via a surgical incision in the neck.

'I don't think it's epiglottitis,' Rafe said. 'He's not drooling and, if anything, he's less distressed than he was a minute ago. Being upright is obviously helping.'

He was, in fact, looking as if he was almost falling asleep again.

'Is he going…to be okay?' Susan was the one sounding distressed now. 'I should have… brought him in before…'

'He's better than I thought he might be,' Rafe told her. 'But I think he needs to go to hospital with you, so that the paediatric team can keep an eye on him for a while. The airways in young children like Dylan are so much smaller than ours so they can start having difficulty breathing quite suddenly when they have a chest infection.' He turned back to Isobel. 'His lung sounds are more in the lower fields and not exactly what I'd expect with croup.'

Isobel nodded. 'So just oxygen for now then, if his saturation is below ninety two percent? No nebuliser, adrenaline or corticosteroids.'

'No…' Rafe handed her the finger clip attached to the small oxygen saturation meter, his eyebrows raised. 'Have you become a paediatric specialist nurse in the last few years?'

'No.' Isobel cuddled Dylan closer. 'Can I

put this on your finger, darling? It doesn't hurt, I promise.' She glanced up at Rafe. 'I retrained,' she told him. 'I've kept my nursing registration up to date and pick up occasional shifts in ED or as a flight care nurse but I'm also a critical care paramedic now.' She glanced down at the screen on the meter. 'Saturation's ninety four percent,' she said.

Rafe continued attaching a mask to an oxygen cylinder. He held it over Susan's mouth and nose as he slipped the elastic band over her head and then tightened it to fit.

'This should help with your breathing,' he told her.

Deb put her head around the door of the treatment room. 'The ambulance is on its way,' she informed them. 'And I've spoken to your mum, Susan. She's on her way here as well.'

Deb sounded anxious and the glance in Rafe's direction was a plea for help, although she kept her voice calm. 'We've got some less than happy people in the waiting room,' she told him. 'Perhaps I should start cancelling appointments?'

Rafe could see that Susan was less short of

breath already. And Dylan was sound asleep in Isobel's arms.

'Could you stay here and monitor Dylan and his mum until the ambulance arrives?' he asked. 'I'd better go and see if there's anything urgent in our waiting room.'

'Of course.' She looked down at the sleeping child in her arms. 'I wasn't planning on disturbing this little guy before I had to.'

Rafe crouched in front of Susan's chair, holding her gaze so that she could see how confident he was that, although she needed extra help right now, both she and Dylan were going to be fine. He held her wrist to check her heart rate and could actually feel her pulse slowing a little with the reassurance.

'I'm not far away,' he told her. 'And Belle's more than qualified to look after you both.'

'I can see that.' Susan was managing a smile beneath the mask. 'We'll be fine, Dr Tanner. I'm sure there are people out there who need you more than we do at the moment.'

Oh, wow...

The way Rafe had been looking at his patient as if her wellbeing and that of her baby were the most important things on his mind. That aura of caring had been as palpable as the warmth of a snuggly blanket and his confidence would inspire trust in anyone. He was the kind of general practitioner that everybody wanted, wasn't he? No wonder this medical practice was obviously so popular and that waiting room so incredibly crowded.

With the ambulance pulling out from the rear of the clinic buildings, Susan and Dylan safely tucked up inside, Isobel headed towards the reception area where she'd dropped her bag when she'd first reached to take Dylan from his panicked mother's arms.

Deb, the receptionist, was dealing with an angry man.

'I took time off work to come here. I'm losing money with every minute I'm hanging around in here and it's just a routine blood test that I had an *appointment* for. I've been waiting for nearly an hour and it's not bloody good enough.'

'I know, I'm so sorry, Mr Jamieson. We've had a bit of an emergency here.'

'That's not my fault.' The man's voice rose. 'It's not as if I even need to see a doctor, it's only the nurse I had an appointment with.'

A woman with a baby was also standing at the counter. 'I've got an appointment with the nurse too, to get my blood pressure checked. I can't wait that long. I've got another appointment to get to.'

'Don't try jumping the queue,' someone seated in the waiting room called out. 'We're all in the same boat. I'm waiting for an ECG.'

Someone else laughed. 'Reckon we'll all have blood pressure problems before too long.'

'I'm sorry,' Deb repeated. 'Our practice nurse is unavailable and we're having trouble replacing her. You *will* be seen as soon as possible. One of the doctors will do your blood test, Mr Jamieson. And check your blood pressure, Mrs Allsop.'

'It won't be soon enough.' The man had his fists clenched. 'I'm leaving. And I'll be making a complaint about this.'

Rafe had come from the corridor leading to the consulting rooms and picked up a file from the basket on the end of the reception desk, clearly about to call for his next patient, but he'd heard what was being said.

'Mr Jamieson? What's the problem?'

'This place is a circus, that's the problem.

No wonder it's called a "practice". Maybe one day you'll actually get good at doing the job properly.'

'Waiting time is getting longer,' Deb told Rafe. 'Especially for the appointments like routine blood pressure checks that need to be slotted in with the doctors, with no nurse available.'

Isobel watched as Rafe glanced over his shoulder at the crowded waiting area before looking back at the man in front of him. It wasn't just the concerned frown creasing his face that caught Isobel, it was the way he unconsciously lifted his hand to rub the back of his neck. A sure sign that he was thinking fast in order to deal with a difficult situation.

She knew that because she'd seen it many times before, often in the context of an emergency department that was experiencing the same kind of chaos that this medical centre had been plunged into this morning. It felt like a step back in time. It also felt impossible not to offer to help.

'I could do Mr Jamieson's blood test,' she told Rafe. 'And take blood pressures and do twelve lead ECGs.'

'Are you sure? Don't you have other things you were planning to do?'

'I've got an appointment with Mum's solicitor but that's not until four o'clock this afternoon. I said I'd go to NICU and spend time with Daisy, but I could do that afterwards. And I can ring the insurance company any time.' It actually felt good to be making a plan for her day and not simply responding to events or emotions. 'So, yes... I'm sure.'

The receptionist's eyebrows had been rising as she listened to their rapid exchange.

'It's okay, Deb,' Rafe said. 'I've worked with Isobel before at St Luke's. She's a well qualified nurse. And a paramedic.' He turned back to Isobel. 'Are you still registered with the Nursing and Midwifery Council in the UK?'

Isobel nodded. 'I just kept it going,' she told him. 'In case I ever needed to come home.'

Except it wasn't home any longer. So why did she feel so comfortable in this place, with the accents of her childhood around her and a medical environment that she was perfectly confident she could cope with?

'You could check online with the NMC,' Rafe told Deb, 'if you want to check Isobel's

credentials, but I'd be more than happy to accept her offer to help this morning.'

'Oh, stop faffing around.' Mr Jamieson was
glaring at Isobel. 'If you're capable of taking a blood test, let's just get on with it, shall
we? I'm about ready to stick the needle in my
own arm.'

Isobel caught Rafe's glance.

'Come with me,' he said. 'I'll show you
the nurse's room and give you a quick ori-
entation.'

There was a gleam in his eyes as he opened
a door next to the treatment room a moment
later. 'You might want to check Mr Jamieson's blood pressure as well,' he murmured.
'Good luck. And thank you.' A corner of his
mouth had a wry curve to it. 'I'm rather glad
I forgot my phone this morning.'

CHAPTER SIX

'I WAS STARTING to get worried about you.'

Yes… Isobel could see the concern on Rafe's face as he turned to see her entering the kitchen that evening. How long was it, she wondered, since she'd seen someone genuinely concerned, on a personal level, about her welfare? It gave her a glow of something warm. Something rather nice. Something that instantly tapped back into that dream she'd once had, of having someone to care about her like this for the rest of her life. Someone that she cared about just as much in return.

The someone that she thought she'd found in Raphael Tanner that night when he'd sat down to talk to her and check that she was okay after they'd been unable to save the patient they'd worked on so hard together. Clearing her throat was also an attempt to clear that ghost of a memory that needed to be avoided. Rafe might have said that she'd been the one he'd loved but that was it in a nutshell, wasn't it?

The past tense.

Don't look back, she reminded herself. *It's not the direction you're going in now.*

'Sorry, Rafe.' Isobel needed a quick breath to steady her voice. 'I should have let you know. I didn't think I'd be this late back but I actually fell asleep doing the kangaroo care with Daisy and the nurses didn't want to disturb either of us. Apparently that's the longest she's been off CPAP with all her vital signs staying within normal parameters. Even her oxygen saturation levels didn't drop enough to set off any alarms.'

'That's great news.' Rafe clicked shut the lunchboxes he'd been filling. 'She's getting stronger.'

'She's even put on a tiny bit of weight. That's another reason they didn't want to wake me up. Apparently the calories saved by being asleep and contented can contribute to weight gain.'

'Speaking of calories, I saved you some dinner. It's in the oven. Nothing very exciting, sorry—just bangers and mash, because I was cooking and it's the boys' favourite.'

'Oh…thank you, but I grabbed a sandwich as I went past the hospital cafeteria. I'd love a cup of tea, but I can make that. Are the boys asleep already?'

'I certainly hope so.' Rafe stored the lunchboxes in the fridge. 'I put them to bed an hour ago. And you sit down. I'll make the tea. I'm still in your debt from this morning.'

Isobel sank onto a chair at the old table at the working end of the kitchen near the Aga. Not only was someone concerned about her wellbeing, he wanted to take care of her on a physical level as well. She'd lived on her own for so long that this felt like a new experience to come home to and that warm glow, deep in her gut, got a little brighter.

Because it was Rafe who was doing the caring?

She put her shoulder bag on the floor beside her, the patch of brown wool beneath the open zip catching her eye as she did so. She pulled out the little teddy bear, putting it on the table in front of her.

'I was going to leave this with Daisy, but I decided I'd better give it a good wash first.

It's really old and probably full of things like dust mites.'

Rafe looked towards her from where he was filling the kettle. 'What is it? A dog?'

'My first teddy bear. I think it might have been Louise from next door who knitted it, and the pattern obviously went a bit wrong, but I still loved it. I gave it to Lauren when she was a baby so I thought Daisy should have it now.'

Rafe sounded surprised. 'And it's something you usually carry around with you in your bag?'

'No...' Isobel let out a huff of laughter. 'I picked it up from the house when I went through with the insurance assessor yesterday. It was about the only thing that looked worth saving.'

The beat of silence between them acknowledged that there were many things Isobel would not want to save from her family home, including the memories of how it had all fallen apart. How her own sister had broken a fundamental rule inherent in family loyalty. How her own mother had failed to defend her. And how her dream of being with the man she loved so much had blown up in her face, along with any conviction that she could ever get any support she needed from her family.

Rafe had a box of milk in his hand but was now staring into the fridge with a thoughtful expression on his face. 'How 'bout a glass of wine instead of that cup of tea? I happen to have a rather nice New Zealand Pinot Gris in here.'

'Oh...'

A bit of time out to really unwind before going to bed and an excuse to linger in this warm, comforting room that was the heart of such a real family home was irresistible. No...it was the thought of turning back time and sharing a glass of wine with just Rafe for company that was really irresistible, wasn't it?

This was probably not the best idea, but Isobel wasn't about to summon the common sense to think about it. Instead, she closed her eyes as she spoke, letting go of any doubts. 'That sounds perfect. It has been rather an eventful day.'

He handed her a glass moments later. He was holding one for himself as well, and he sat down at the end of the table and raised his glass to touch against hers in a toast.

'Thanks again for your help this morning. We would have sunk completely if it hadn't been for you seeing so many people. Your ability to triage and provide us with an initial assessment of vital signs was especially valuable for saving time and clearing the backlog.'

'I really enjoyed it,' Isobel admitted. 'Even having to hunt for so many things, like more ECG dots and where the flu vaccines were stored in the fridge, was good. Oh, you're very low on specimen jars and I used the last urine dipstick this afternoon, but I mentioned it to Deb and she's ordered some more. Hopefully you won't get any more UTIs coming through the door before they arrive.'

Rafe seemed to be listening carefully. 'I did wonder how well Linnda was keeping up with some aspects of her work,' he said, 'but she loved her job so much she wouldn't hear of retiring. I saw her today and she should make a good recovery from the stroke but there's no way she'll be coming back—which could be a blessing in disguise once we've found the right person to fill the gap. You've reminded me of just how many balls need to be juggled and kept in the air at the same time. It takes a particular kind of person to thrive in a stressful job like that.'

'It was exactly what I needed today,' Isobel said. 'I've got so many things that I can't control to worry about at the moment so it was kind of nice to focus on stuff that I know exactly how to manage.' She took an appreciative sip of her wine. 'Stuff that doesn't… I don't know…mess with your head, I guess.'

Rafe didn't say anything but she knew he was still listening. His silence made her think he was waiting for her to say something more. That he *wanted* to hear more? Having someone genuinely interested in what was going on in her life was adding another layer to that feeling of being cared for.

She let her breath out in a sigh this time. 'Everything seems to be getting more complicated. Mum's estate is a bit of a mess to say the least. She didn't leave a will, which means that it would have been divided equally between her children, but Lauren died straight after her and she didn't leave a will either, so that means her half gets divided between her children. All three of them. The solicitor says it'll take quite some time to get sorted and it may have to wait until the house is repaired and valued. Or sold, even.' She took another, longer, sip of her wine. 'And that's another huge question mark. Goodness only knows how long it will be before the house can be valued, let alone go on the market.'

If seemed more and more likely that this process was going to take months. That meant she would definitely have to find somewhere else to stay, but Isobel bit her lip to stop herself saying anything about moving out. Because her heart was sinking at the thought of doing that?

She might have believed she'd never wanted to see Rafe again but it was nowhere near as disturbing as she had expected. It was unsettling, sure, but not in an entirely unpleasant way. And she loved this house. This kitchen. The feeling of life that came with two small boys and quite a large dog sharing the space. She had to admit that a large part of her didn't want to move out any time soon. Especially when Rafe was looking at her as if he really cared about whatever was messing with her head.

It was a bit like being in some strange hall of mirrors where reality got twisted. This was like a glimpse into the life she could have had, if that Christmas party had worked out the way she'd hoped it would. If she and Rafe had both realised that they couldn't see their future without sharing it with each other and had reignited their romance that night.

'Is there anything I can do to help?'

Oh...that was a question and a half, wasn't it? Could he turn back time, perhaps, and make all that devastation disappear? Make the family feel of this house and kitchen and children and dog the real heart of her current life? No... Of course he couldn't.

Isobel shook her head. 'You've done enough. It's me who should be thanking you for everything you've done already, like organising the funeral. That can't have been easy given how badly my sister—and my mother, by the sound of it—treated you.'

Rafe's shrug suggested that it wasn't something he intended dwelling on. That it had only been the right thing to do, perhaps, but another thought had suddenly occurred to Isobel.

'I must owe you a small fortune for the funeral costs. There's no reason you should have to foot that bill for your ex-wife.'

Rafe shook his head. 'Forget it. It was something I needed to do for my own conscience,' he said quietly. 'A token apology?' He rubbed the back of his neck, his gaze dropping. 'I didn't try hard enough to make things work. When I wasn't at the hospital, I was looking after the babies. I knew Lauren wasn't happy so I didn't blame her for leaving—I was just grateful she hadn't taken my boys. It was never a real marriage. We never even shared a bedroom...'

Oh, dear Lord... Isobel studied the last few drops of liquid in her wine glass. She didn't need that kind of intimate detail of what had gone on in his marriage to her sister. It was doing something odd to her body, like the way hearing him say that he had once loved her had done. She drained the last drops of her wine from the glass, carefully avoiding catching Rafe's gaze. She didn't want him to see what might be showing in her own eyes. Not when it could be something that could scare herself as much as him.

He got to his feet and, thankfully, it felt like a signal that the subject was closed.

'I could help with keeping an eye on the house repairs,' he offered as he came back from the fridge with the wine bottle in his hand. 'If you need to go back to New Zealand for a while.'

'I've told people I'm unavailable for any shifts for a month or so. And someone's keeping an eye on my apartment. I'll have to make other arrangements if I'm staying longer than that, but there's bigger things than my job to think about.'

This time the silence between them felt even more loaded. Rafe sat down again, caught her gaze and then held it, nodding slowly. That concern for her was there in his face again, along with a sincere empathy in those dark eyes.

'Daisy,' he said quietly.

Isobel could feel the prickle of tears gathering behind her eyes. That he understood that bond with a baby that could come from nowhere and hit with such strength gave them a new connection. It gave her the impression that he was on her side and wasn't about to make any judgements on whatever she was feeling. The kind of support that a family could provide but something she'd never been able to rely on.

'Maybe it was a mistake giving her a name,'

she confessed. 'It felt so different today. As if…as if…'

'As if she's yours?'

The suggestion was just as quiet but carried all the understanding in the world and Isobel nodded just as slowly as he just had. She could feel a tear escaping at the same time and brushed it away with her fingers.

'It's too big,' she whispered. 'And I don't know what I'm going to do.'

'You don't have to know yet. Or do anything other than take one day at a time right now,' Rafe told her. 'You'll know when you know. What you *are* doing is being there for her and helping her to get stronger and…and that's a very special thing to be able to do.' He nudged the little brown teddy bear on the table between them. 'This is special too, in its own unique way.' He smiled. 'I'll bet it becomes something very precious for Daisy. A family heirloom.'

Isobel smiled through her tears. 'A rather wonky one.'

Rafe's smile widened. 'Perfection is overrated.'

He refilled her wine glass. 'New Zealand makes some great wine,' he said. 'I'd love to visit the place one day. Maybe a campervan trip with the boys when they're old enough to appreciate it. I'd better pick your brains while you're here and make a list of all the "must-see" places.'

'It'll be a long list,' Isobel said. 'I've been there for years and feel like I've barely scratched the surface, even working on helicopters for a while and being able to fly into some of the top tourist spots, like the national parks.'

Rafe's phone beeped as she finished speaking and she watched the frown line appear between his eyes. He glanced up a heartbeat later, as if he'd been able to feel the touch of her concerned gaze.

'It's the locum agency,' he told her. 'They're working late, obviously, but they haven't been able to find a practice nurse for us that can start immediately. End of the week at the earliest.' He shook his head and put his phone back in his shirt pocket. 'Dealing with that can wait till the morning.' He took a mouthful of his wine. 'It sounds like you have an exciting job. Where are you based at the moment?'

'My apartment's in Queenstown. I have casual employment with both the ambulance service and the local hospital, which is great because I get to pick my hours but it may be a while before a permanent position anywhere gets advertised. It's a popular place to live.'

'I can imagine. That's *Lord of the Rings* country, isn't it? Spectacular mountains and lakes and forests and lots of snow in winter?'

'It's gorgeous. I love it.'

'And have you got family there?'

Isobel blinked at him. He knew perfectly well that she'd just lost her only family members.

The expression on Rafe's face suggested embarrassment. Or an apology? 'I meant, you know…a husband. Or kids, even.'

'Oh…' Fair enough. She'd thought that Helen was Rafe's new wife, hadn't she? And that he had added a couple of kids to his own brood in the time she'd been out of the country.

She took a much larger sip of her wine. 'No. On both counts.'

It felt as if she was admitting to some kind of failure. It wasn't that she hadn't tried to find a special person to share her life with. She'd dated quite a few men over the years, but it never seemed to go anywhere. She changed jobs, or spent too much time on shift work, or…there just hadn't been enough to build on.

Or, maybe, she'd been trying to find someone that made her feel exactly the same way that Raphael Tanner had and there would only ever be one man who could do that. That, perhaps, it was preferable to live with the loneliness than in a relationship where it was so obvious that something important was missing.

'I'm footloose and fancy free, really.' She could hear the unnaturally bright tone to her voice. She needed to change the subject so she added the first thing she could think of. 'Apart from keeping up rental payments in one of the priciest real estate areas in the country.' She bit her lip as she remembered worrying about finances earlier today, when she was talking to the solicitor dealing with her mother's estate. 'There'll be costs I have to keep up on Mum's house until it gets sold too. I might need to find a budget hotel when you've had enough of your life being disrupted by an uninvited visitor.' She managed a wry smile. 'Maybe it's just as well I still have current nursing registration. You never know, I might end up looking for a job while I'm here.'

'Well, what do you know? I happen to know about a job you'd be perfect for. At the Harrison Street Medical Centre.'

The words had come out of Rafe's mouth before he'd really thought about them. Maybe it was some kind of protective mechanism to cover up what he was *really* thinking about. That Isobel was single. That there was nothing to anchor her on the other side of the world, other than a job.

There would be many, many jobs available for someone with her abilities right here in Balclutha. And that would mean he could see more of her. There could be other occasions when he could sit and share a glass of wine with her and talk about life and...

And be reminded, yet again, of how he'd stuffed up the best thing that had ever happened to him? That surprised expression currently on Isobel's face could quickly morph into wariness, couldn't it? What was he thinking? And after he'd suggested the wine instead of a cup of tea to try and soften the unpleasantness of their shared memories.

He pasted a grin onto his face. 'Just kidding... I know you've got more than enough demands on your time right now. But you were brilliant this morning. You even picked up what was probably a silent myocardial infarction on old Mrs Maloney when you spotted the changes on her routine ECG. No wonder she's been so short of breath lately.'

Isobel didn't seem to register the praise. She was looking thoughtful rather than pleased.

'Are you looking for a full-time practice nurse?' she asked. 'Because if it was part-time I'd have time to spend with Daisy every day and there'll be other things I have to do, I expect. Like decisions for the house and legal stuff.'

Rafe stared at her. 'Would you really consider it?'

Was this a step in the wrong direction? It would mean spending even more time in Isobel's company. Working with her, in fact, which was how they'd met in the first place. Did he want to do that?

No.

Yes...

'The hours you worked today were great,' Rafe said. 'I know everybody would be thrilled if you could do that Monday to Friday. And I'm in charge of employing someone so we can figure out what would work best for you. But…are you sure?'

'I meant it when I said how good it had been today to be able to focus on stuff that's easy to handle. It almost felt like I had a bit of control over my life which has been rather lacking lately. Having a routine would probably be even better. But are *you* sure? Was today typical for what your practice nurse needs to be able to do?'

Was he sure?

Not exactly. He was confused, to be honest. There were feelings being stirred that he'd successfully kept buried for a very long time. He'd said too much already too, not just telling Isobel that she'd been the one he'd loved but admitting that he'd only ever slept with her sister that one time. He'd thought he'd lost everything he'd ever had with Isobel Matthews. He hadn't even expected her to turn up to the funeral, let alone that she would be staying in his house but, now that she was here, he was remembering just how much he *had* lost.

Was it remotely possible that some of the good things he remembered from their relationship were still there?

It had felt like that when he'd seen her sitting with Daisy on her bare skin. When he'd remembered with such bittersweet clarity what it had been like when he'd fallen in love with this woman. And it had felt like it this evening, when he'd wanted to take care of her. To reassure and support her.

They couldn't go back, he knew that. He didn't expect to be forgiven, if they could ever get to the point of talking honestly about what had happened, but a step towards understanding would surely be worthwhile. It could bring some sort of peace, perhaps, and create a foundation for friendship, even? What if something important was still alive between them, even if it was only there because of the bond they had by their relationships with and through Oscar and Josh and Daisy? It could be deeper than friendship. The kind of caring that would make them part of the same family and…yes…that was worth nurturing.

He *was* sure about that.

'Absolutely.' He nodded to emphasise his response. 'The job description includes the ability to assist with emergencies like resuscitation and stabilisation, which we both know you're more than qualified for with your experience in ED and as a paramedic.'

Isobel echoed his nod. 'I've done advanced resuscitation training.'

'There's admin stuff like following up test results and communicating with patients, acting as a chaperone if needed, assisting with minor surgery and what you were doing today with taking vital signs, doing blood tests and vaccinations et cetera. Oh, and home visits too, if they're required. We're one of a dying breed of medical centres that provides home visits from both doctors and the practice nurse. The doctors are on a roster to cover each day and I do mine on Tuesdays and Fridays between lunch and afternoon surgery.' His smile was wry. 'Sometimes instead of lunch. I eat my sandwiches while I'm driving.'

'I'm used to that too. I've done twelve-hour shifts on ambulance where it felt like a luxury to be able to go to the loo.'

He could imagine that. He knew how dedicated Isobel could be to her work. To everything she chose to include in her life, for that matter. If she chose to do it, she would give it everything she had. And then a bit more.

'The main attribute we'd be looking for,

aside from medical qualifications, is the ability to troubleshoot. To make intelligent decisions and be able to recognise who needs urgent additional care. You're overqualified in all respects, of course, but it would be a godsend for us, even if it's only temporary.'

A flush of pink was colouring Isobel's cheeks and the look in her eyes touched something deep in his gut. She was looking as if his praise really meant something. As if she was proud of herself because he was the one telling her how good she was?

'How 'bout you try it for a few days and see how it goes?' Rafe suggested. 'If it doesn't look like it's going to work, we can try someone else from the locum agency next week.'

But, if it did work, it would keep Isobel close. It could build a new foundation for the unusual family group they were both part of.

'Forget about finding a hotel,' he added, trying to sound as if it was no big deal. 'Budget or otherwise. If it does work, you could consider room and board a part of the job package if that helps. Oscar and Josh are so thrilled to have their new aunty here. They think you're the best thing since sliced bread. Especially since I told them you can drive an ambulance. Giving them the chance to get to know you is an unexpected bonus to come out of a very unfortunate situation.'

'It's a bonus for me too,' Isobel said. 'They're gorgeous kids, Rafe. A real credit to you. I'm just sorry I haven't been part of their lives so far. I've got a bit of making up to do, haven't I?'

'Kids can be astonishingly forgiving.' Rafe shared the last of the wine between their glasses. 'We can probably learn something from them in that regard.'

Maybe it was the mention of forgiveness that did it. Or the idea that Isobel was prepared to make an effort to repair damage on his side of the equation. Whatever it was, he could feel a prickle of what had to be tears at the back of his eyes.

He raised his glass. 'It's been a long time, Belle.' He blinked back any embryonic tears but that didn't make the feeling that went with them disappear.

Relief? Hope…?

His voice softened. 'If we wanted it to be, this could be a fresh start for us as well.'

Isobel's heart skipped a beat and then accelerated as she touched his glass again and then took what turned out to be more of a gulp than a sip of the wine. Was he talking about a fresh start that involved them being together again? In the wake of his ex-wife's funeral? Her *sister's* funeral? *No*…she already had far too much to deal with emotionally. This was just another reflection in those weird reality-distorting mirrors. She might be having some confusing memories and glimpses of what could have been—possibly could still be—but she couldn't afford to give them any real head space because they held an undercurrent of very real fear.

The fear of feeling that depth of love for someone and the hopes and dreams of a future together because she knew the flip side—the devastation when it was ripped away, leaving a heart, and life, torn and bleeding. She couldn't willingly volunteer to go through that again and, if she thought that Rafe was issuing an invitation, she would most likely run for the hills. She could actually feel her muscles tensing, ready to act on a flight or fight reflex.

But she knew Rafe would never be that insensitive. He probably had no idea how much of what he felt showed on his face and in his actions. Like how much he adored his sons.

The way he cared about his patients. That genuine understanding about the life-changing bombshell addition to her life that a small, fragile baby in NICU was presenting.

And what she could see on his face right now was an expression that was reassuring rather than inviting. For a moment, when he'd made the suggestion of a fresh start, she'd thought she'd seen the glimmer of tears in his eyes—as if it meant something very significant—but that had gone now.

And he might have admitted that he'd loved her rather than Lauren, but he'd also just reminded her that it had been a very long time ago. It was part of a past that no longer existed and perhaps what he was really suggesting was that they both put it behind them and start again with simply a clean slate. That was fine with Isobel. A relief, in fact. She could feel the tension in her muscles subsiding.

This was a professional proposal. One that happened to also offer a way to turn back time on an emotional level. To return to a time when they had worked together and had formed a genuine friendship before becoming lovers. A chance to push a 'reset' button and, yes…have a fresh start.

And it was purely professional, which made it feel…safe.

It was a job tailored to suit both her qualifications and her available hours. Free accommodation thrown in. Staying here could provide a solid base—along with the company of someone who had just demonstrated that he cared about her wellbeing—that would undoubtably make it much easier to deal with difficult times in the weeks to come.

Yes. The whole package felt solid and safe. The kind of rock that Isobel desperately needed to cling to right now, given that the familiar foundation of her life had just been whipped out from beneath her feet. Her family was gone and her future hung in the balance, given that if she chose to raise Daisy, going back to the life she had created for herself in the last few years would be totally impossible.

But she didn't need to think about that in this moment. As Rafe had said, all she needed to do for now was what she was doing. One day at a time. Today had made it very clear that being able to plan her days to include using her medical skills in a job she loved could only be a good thing for everyone concerned. Those few hours of being totally focused on patients had provided her with a means to help silence the overload of personal emotional stuff she was having to process as well as a chance to escape the draining thought spirals of the biggest things, like the future for herself and Daisy or the past for herself and Rafe. Having had that break had enabled her to simply be in the moment with Daisy, which could well have been why they'd both ended up in a contented nap. Building a break like that into almost every day would be better for everyone concerned.

Especially herself.

With how long the house repairs were going to take, she actually had plenty of time to consider what was going to be the best option for herself and Daisy going forward. And she could banish her past history with Rafe back into that secure part of her brain because this was a fresh start and it was all about the present. About the children who linked them. And a new professional relationship.

The relief was becoming so palpable Isobel found herself smiling at Rafe, in fact. 'I'd better get to bed,' she said. 'It seems like I've got work in the morning.'

CHAPTER SEVEN

'Rafe?'

Rafe didn't need to glance at his dashboard to confirm that it was Isobel calling. Somehow, in the last couple of weeks, he had become familiar enough again with her voice to know that this was her professional tone. Which was entirely appropriate, given that it was the middle of a working day. What wasn't quite so appropriate, perhaps, was how much of a pleasure it was to hear her voice.

It might only have been a short time since Isobel had joined the staff at Harrison Street Medical Centre, but it had worked remarkably well right from day one and there'd been no question of getting the locum agency to find them another contender. Rafe had known she would be good at doing this job, but he hadn't realised quite *how* good, and he was proud of her. He also liked the feeling that, at least on one level, they were managing to turn back time to a point where they'd been colleagues. Friends. And it still felt safe enough.

'What's up, Belle?'

'Are you at work at the moment?'

'No, I'm on the road. I've got a home visit to do.'

'Is it urgent?'

'Not particularly. A potential bedsore to assess. Why?'

'I'm on a home visit. With Albert Morris.'

Rafe frowned. 'Type Two diabetic?'

'That's him. He didn't sound too bad when he rang to ask for an appointment this morning. He's been off colour for quite a few days, very thirsty, frequent urination and a bit "fuzzy", he called it. Said he'd run out of test strips for his glucometer, but he sounded a bit confused and I'm not happy about his condition. I think I should call an ambulance.'

Rafe had pulled to the side of the road to focus on what Isobel was telling him.

'Signs and symptoms?'

'Airway's clear but resps are up at thirty. He's tachycardic at one thirty and his blood pressure's one-oh-five over sixty-five. He's very dehydrated. Skin tenting and his eyes look sunken. Blood glucose level is too high to record. His temperature's thirty-eight point two and I found blood in his urine when I did a dipstick.'

'Ketones?'

'No.'

'Not diabetic ketoacidosis then, which I wouldn't expect, anyway, unless he's a Type One diabetic.'

'No. I can't smell any ketones on his breath and he hasn't complained about abdominal pain or vomiting but I'm wondering about HHS. I've noticed a few ectopic beats but I can't do an ECG here. A urinary tract infection could be the cause and he's obviously confused. He couldn't tell me what day it was or how old he is.'

Hyperosmolar Hyperglycaemic Syndrome. Just as dangerous as DKA in that it could lead to coma or death due to cardiac complications from electrolyte imbalances.

'Where are you?' Rafe asked.

The address Isobel gave him wasn't that far from where Rafe was himself. 'I've got a life pack with me,' he told her. 'Call an ambulance but it probably doesn't need to be a Priority One response. I'll drop in and we'll get an ECG. We can upgrade the request if we need to but he should be monitored for hyperkalaemic arrhythmias that could develop.'

It took Rafe less than ten minutes to reach the address where Albert Morris lived but it had been enough time for the condition of the seventy-two-year-old man to deteriorate.

''Bout time you got here,' Albert mumbled. He was sitting slumped on his couch. 'But you can leave your dog outside. I don't want hair all over my furniture.'

'No problem.' Rafe raised an eyebrow at Isobel. Hallucinations? His query was silent but Isobel nodded.

'I had to shoo the invisible cats out a few minutes ago,' she whispered.

'I'll get an IV in,' Rafe said. 'Fluid replacement is going to be a priority for treatment here. Can you do an ECG?'

'Sure.' Isobel uncoiled the leads from the side pocket of the life pack but spoke to their patient before opening his pyjama jacket to attach the electrodes.

'I need to put some sticky patches on your chest, Albert, so we can see what your heart's up to. Is that okay with you?'

'You can do whatever you like to me, darling.' Albert closed his eyes. 'I'm thirsty... I think there's a beer in my fridge. Could you get it for me?'

'In a minute,' Isobel murmured. 'I'm just going to do this first, okay?'

Rafe slipped a tourniquet around Albert's arm, having unrolled his IV kit. 'Keep your arm as still as you can,' he warned their patient. 'Sharp scratch coming up.'

He kept well out of Isobel's way as she opened Albert's pyjama jacket and stuck electrodes for the limb leads below his collarbones and above the hipbones. Then she quickly placed the precordial leads around his heart, counting intercostal spaces by feeling for the ribs and gauging the vertical lines by sight. As Rafe slid the cannula into a vein and secured it, Isobel was attaching the leads to the electrodes and watching the screen of the life pack to make sure the connections were good.

'Keep nice and still for me, Albert,' she said, putting her hand on his shoulder too. 'I'm going to take a picture of what that ticker of yours is up to.'

She was smiling at the older man, who might well be confused and even hallucinating at times but he was clearly captured enough by Isobel's smile to lie very still and simply smile back for as long as it took the machine to record the electrical activity going on and print out a graph for them to see. And that didn't surprise Rafe one little bit. He could remember being just as entranced with smiles that Isobel Matthews had bestowed on him, long ago. Smiles that could light up the world and make it a better place. The best place...

He pushed the spike of a giving set into the port on the bag of saline he was holding with slightly more force than necessary but it was a deliberate action to stop his mind spending any more than a nanosecond on that train of thought. Because he knew it would lead into an out-of-bounds space—the space where he could remember, with more and more ease, what it had been like to be falling in love with Isobel—when he'd known she was already in love with him, even though nothing had been said out loud.

Was it because it felt safe to be working together again and making that fresh start, that it was becoming a little too easy to step into that unwise space? Ironically, because they were working together, it was equally easy to step out of that space and push the thought firmly away. As he attached the tubing of the IV fluid to the line in Albert's arm and adjusted the rate of infusion, Rafe was keeping an eye on the screen on the life pack, completely focused again. The rhythm trace was somewhat irregular and was being interrupted quite frequently by the bizarre shape of premature beats—a warning sign that things weren't stable and could potentially deteriorate into a fatal rhythm and cardiac arrest.

Isobel handed him the recorded trace. 'Peaked T waves, wide QRS and diminished P waves. All consistent with a high potassium level.'

Rafe nodded. 'And there's no ST elevation so we can rule out a heart attack.'

'Shall I upgrade the urgency of the ambulance call?'

'Let's see if we can get that rhythm a bit more settled first.' Rafe turned back to his kit to take out the drug roll. 'How would you treat this as a critical care paramedic?' he asked.

'IV calcium chloride to stabilise cardiac membrane potential,' Isobel responded. 'It lasts thirty to sixty minutes, which is usually plenty of time to get to an ED where treatment with insulin and glucose can happen. Nebulised albuterol is also useful to shift potassium into the intracellular space.'

'Sodium bicarbonate?' Rafe was drawing up fluid from an ampoule into a syringe but he glanced up to catch the gleam in Isobel's eyes. She knew he was testing her but she didn't mind.

'Not unless the patient's in known acidosis,' she said. 'As I'm sure you're aware, Dr Tanner.'

She turned away, hiding a smile. 'You're doing well, Albert. You're going to feel a lot better soon, I promise.'

The calcium chloride had an almost immediate effect on the rhythm of Albert's heart, with the ectopic beats starting to get less frequent. Minutes later, the ambulance arrived and Albert was soon on a stretcher and ready for transport.

'But I haven't had my beer,' he complained. 'I'm still thirsty.'

'It'll be here for you when you get home,' Isobel told him. 'And I'll be back to check on you.'

'Any time, darling.' Albert lay back on his

pillow and closed his eyes as the stretcher was rolled away. 'Any time…'

There was no time to waste packing up the life pack and kit and Isobel was onto it.

'Sorry to have held you up but I'm so glad you were here. I'd hate to have had to deal with an arrest on my own without any gear.'

Rafe was going to be pushed to visit his patient with the bedsore before he needed to be back at Harrison Street for the afternoon surgery hours, but he was just as glad he'd been able to be here.

'I think we should make sure you've got a full resuscitation kit available, given that your skill level is well above the average practice nurse. But let's talk about that tonight. I've really got to get going.'

Rafe was perfectly confident that they would talk about it tonight because it was becoming a familiar—and increasingly pleasant—end to most of their evenings to share a cup of tea or sometimes a glass of wine and talk about their days, which often led to talking about snippets of their lives in recent years. Josh couldn't get enough of hearing about cases where Isobel had been winched out of a helicopter or had to drive on precarious mountain roads to reach a patient. Rafe wasn't sure if it was a need to fill in the gaps of what had been happening in her life since she'd left or whether he was searching for things that had changed and made her different or trying to rediscover the things that hadn't changed—the things he'd loved about her right from the start, but it wasn't a problem because it felt safe.

An even bigger question might be whether that was what Isobel was also doing when she asked questions about what it had been like being a single father and his rather dramatic change of career from the fast pace of a busy emergency department to the far more predictable routine of a general practice. Perhaps they both needed this time to get to know each other again. Laying foundations that could provide a base for something important, like a genuine friendship and an extended family for Oscar and Josh. It felt as if they were building trust that clearly hadn't been there enough in the first place because it had been too easily broken—on both sides.

It was a time alone together that was feeling that bit safer with every day that passed, despite those unexpected steps into the forbidden space. Not safe enough yet to step onto ground that had been shelved by mutual consent, but it wasn't unthinkable that they might close some of that distance between them one of these days by talking about their shared past.

But not just yet. They needed this safe space to get to know each other again. To build trust. And Rafe wanted to remember what it had been like when they'd first met. When they'd been colleagues. Friends. Before things had spiralled into something intense enough to be overwhelming for him. Before he'd pulled the plug on something that he wasn't ready to trust enough. Before he'd messed things up to the point where he'd lost the chance of the relationship he later knew he'd wanted far more than he'd realised.

It wasn't just Rafe and Isobel that needed that safe space either. Even more, there were two small boys who needed to be protected.

Isobel hadn't been wrong in thinking that a routine, including a job, would help her navigate what was probably the most difficult period she had faced in her life so far. Okay, *definitely* the most difficult, but it took some doing to knock the memory of how hard it had been to travel as far away as she could get on earth and start a completely new life, when it had felt like her broken heart was unlikely to ever heal, from its top position on that scale.

It had only taken a matter of days for her new routine to become familiar enough to reveal that it was going to be beneficial on more levels than simply providing a structure to her days. Things were chaotic enough to block any personal thought spirals that threatened to create emotional overload and, by the end of each day, Isobel was tired enough to fall into a dreamless sleep.

The chaos began each day in the company of the twins and Cheddar, there was the surprisingly satisfying work as a practice nurse that kept her focused from nine o'clock till three o'clock—with her lunch break being used to keep up with what was happening with the structural work to repair her mother's house and the plans that needed to be made for renovations. Then there was the time with Daisy, between work and getting home to Rafe's house for dinner, that was falling into its own routine of feeding and doing the kangaroo care and it was going to be extended soon to include a bath as her tiny niece continued to grow and get bigger and stronger.

Isobel was sure that Daisy was coming to recognise her as a special person in her life. She didn't fall asleep so often during their time of snuggling skin-to-skin and Isobel would find dark eyes locked on her face. It felt almost like a secret language they were communicating in as that eye contact remained unbroken for such long periods of time.

Sometimes she was too late to share dinner with Rafe and the boys, but she was always back by seven o'clock because it had also become an important part of her routine to hear Oscar and Josh's reading homework, admire any new artwork and maybe play a game if there was time before the bedtime story with their dad.

And then came the part of Isobel's day that she was starting to look forward to the most. The quiet half hour or so where she and Rafe shared a drink and chatted about the day.

'The insurance company is covering new furniture and curtains after all the mouldy stuff had to be thrown out,' she told him one day. 'Look what I found online today—I just love these reproduction brass beds. You can get patchwork quilts to go with them.'

'Nice.'

'The better the house looks when it's finished, the quicker it will sell. Any furniture can be sold with it, I expect.'

On another day, Rafe had been in to see Daisy.

'I'm sure she's smiling. Look, I took a photo.'

'Could be wind.' Had Isobel been jealous that Rafe might have been given Daisy's first smile?

'Oscar and Josh reckon she's smiling. They're dead keen to meet their sister but I've told them they'll have to wait a bit longer. There's a few bugs going around at school at the moment and we can't risk taking them into NICU.'

Sometimes it was a purely professional discussion, like going over the details of their management of Albert Morris the other day and sharing any follow up. Albert's infection had been brought under control, along with his blood sugar and electrolyte levels, and Isobel would be able to do another home visit very soon and make sure he was managing his new glucometer. The benefits of her having a life pack in her own vehicle for home visits was already on the agenda for the next medical centre staff meeting.

And, every time, there was the sheer pleasure of simply being in Rafe's company. Listening to his voice and waiting to see that smile she'd always loved. And okay...if she let herself drift off to stand in front of one of those mirrors, that wasn't a problem, was it? It wasn't as if Rafe had any idea that she might be watching his hand lift a mug of tea and remembering what it had been like to have those fingers touching her own skin.

If that memory happened to give her that delicious spear of sensation deep in her belly that went with a level of physical attraction that had been missing from her life for so long, that was okay too, wasn't it? Maybe she needed the reminder of how important something like desire could be? How it could add a colour and vibrancy to the most ordinary things, like sharing a cup of tea? And it was hidden well enough for Rafe to have no idea that those mirrors existed and that made it safe.

Weekends brought more time with Daisy

and more time with the boys and Rafe and it had only taken a couple of outings for walks on the nearest beach to become another new favourite for Isobel. Cheddar would chase seagulls and the boys would fly their kites on windy days or compete with each other to add to their collection of stones with holes in them.

'I believe they're called hag stones,' Rafe told Isobel one Saturday afternoon.

'No…really? That's a horrible name for them. I've always called them bead stones. I collected them when I was kid and threaded them onto a string to hang from a branch in a tree. They might still be there—I'll have a look next time I go to the house.'

'Can we do that, Aunty Belle?' Oscar begged. 'I want to make a string of bead stones.'

'Me too,' Josh added.

'You'll have to find lots more stones, then.'

The boys ran off and it was when Isobel heard the first shriek of glee at a successful find that it happened. So suddenly that Isobel stopped in her tracks and Rafe turned back to look at her.

'What is it? Is something wrong?'

'You were right,' Isobel said slowly.

Rafe grinned. 'Of course I was. What about, exactly?'

'That I would know when I know. About what I want to do?'

Rafe was watching her intently but he wasn't saying anything. Because he knew how big this moment was? It wasn't just what Isobel wanted to *do*. It was what she wanted in her life.

She wanted this.

Family.

Not exactly this one, of course. This was Rafe's. But she did want a family of her own—more than anything she'd ever wanted in her life.

'I'm going to adopt Daisy,' she said, slowly enough to make each word crystal clear.

The boys were well away from them now, scrabbling about amongst the millions of stones on this beach, with Cheddar helpfully trying to dig a hole. Rafe was keeping an eye on them but his gaze returned to Isobel's face and she was startled to see something that looked like disappointment in his eyes. Fear, almost…?

'You'll take her to New Zealand?' he asked quietly.

Isobel shook her head. She also tried to shake off the wild thought that it might be herself that Rafe didn't want to lose from his life, rather than Daisy. This decision was entirely separate to anything to do with any ghosts from the past or possibilities for the future. This was the present and Isobel was about to change the entire shape of her life.

'How could I do that? Daisy has her brothers here. My nephews. She has an uncle. We're part of the same family.' Isobel swallowed hard. She couldn't read the expression in Rafe's eyes any longer. Did he need reassurance that she wasn't expecting something he wasn't able to give?

'I'm the one choosing what Mum's house is going to be like so it's already feeling like it could be my house,' she added. 'I could live there. I mean, New Zealand is a wonderful place but this…this is home…'

Rafe had her in his arms before she'd finished speaking so she was wrapped in his hug as she said those last words.

And, heaven help her, but *this* felt like home as well.

Rafe's voice, right in her ear, sounded raw. 'I'm so happy that you're back,' he said softly. He pulled back just far enough to see her face. 'I've missed you, Belle.'

This time, it was Isobel who couldn't find anything to say. She was totally caught by what she could see in Rafe's eyes. Joy? Relief? *Tears...?*

Whatever it was, she couldn't look away. Neither could Rafe, it seemed. And then something else—possibly as momentous as Isobel's decision had been—happened. Rafe bent his head. Isobel went up on her tiptoes and she closed her eyes as Rafe's lips touched hers.

A kiss that was seasoned with the salt of tears. Rafe's? Or her own? Not that it mattered. This might have only been a brief kiss, but it was the most intense that Isobel had ever experienced. It had all the bittersweet memories of past kisses they'd shared but it had something that was celebrating new beginnings as well.

A huge decision had been made.

Maybe more than one?

CHAPTER EIGHT

IT WAS STILL THERE.

The sea breeze should have been enough to disperse it, given that both Rafe and Isobel could see that it was making the boys' cheeks very pink as Oscar and Josh ran back across the beach towards them, but it was still there.

Hanging in the air between them.

That kiss…

A kiss that had been hidden by Rafe's back and brief enough to have gone unnoticed by the two small boys. A kiss that had simply been a natural extension of a hug to celebrate what was, to Rafe, the amazingly good news that Daisy was going to be raised by the closest family she had. That she wasn't going to end up a world away from her brothers. A kiss that could—and should—have been no big deal.

Except that he had kissed Isobel's lips, not her cheek.

And the touch had not only unlocked that forbidden space full of memories and broken dreams again, it felt as if the key had also been taken out and possibly thrown away. They might be carefully avoiding catching each other's gaze right now but it was inevitable that they were going to have to talk about what had just happened. Rafe was, in fact, almost desperate to know what Isobel was thinking. How she was feeling. Whether she, too, had a space locked away in her heart that was significant enough to make it risky to visit.

Was it possible that she was without a life partner for the same reason as himself? That she'd never found something as good as that, albeit fragile, promise they'd found with each other?

'Your face is all red,' Oscar told Isobel.

'So is yours, darling.' Isobel ducked her head, clearly aware of what might have *really* made her cheeks quite that pink. 'That's what a cold wind can do.'

A heartbeat later, however, Isobel's gaze flicked up to Rafe's face as if she couldn't help herself and there was a sparkle in those blue eyes that he hadn't seen before. No…that wasn't entirely true. He *had* seen it before. Before things had fallen apart. Before he'd made the biggest mistake of his life. The eye contact was even more brief than that kiss had been but it was enough to suggest she wasn't unhappy with what had just happened. The thought that it could be quite the opposite was enough to make Rafe's heart skip a beat and it was his turn to try and hide what he was thinking. This was dangerous ground to be merely looking at, let alone stepping onto.

'Show me what you've found.' Rafe crouched to look at the stones the boys were clutching in their hands.

'Mine are the best,' Josh declared. 'Look at this one.' But it was to Isobel that he handed the smooth oval white stone with a hole just off centre.

'I'm sure I found one just like this,' she said. 'And it was my favourite too. Along with one of those grey ones that's like a little bit of a pipe that you've found, Oscar.'

'Can you show us?'

'I don't know if they'll still be there.' Isobel shook her head and the breeze helped another curl escape her short puff of a ponytail. Rafe watched as she brushed it away from getting tangled in her eyelashes and, heaven help him, if his boys weren't standing right here, he would probably be brushing her hair back himself. And kissing her again...

'It was a long, long time ago,' Isobel added. 'I wasn't much older than you boys are now.'

The twins looked suitably impressed. 'But you're really old. Like Daddy.'

Rafe laughed. 'I'm not that old,' he protested. 'But I am getting *cold*. Are you guys ready to go home?'

They both shook their heads.

'We need more stones. To make a string. Aunty Belle's going to show us how.'

'We do need a couple of sticks of driftwood,' Isobel said. 'To hang the strings from. But we could find them next time, yes?'

Next time... That had a ring to it that was a promise.

Because Isobel would be part of that 'next time'? That bubble of what felt like hope should be more than enough to be a warning. Especially given the expression on his boys' faces as they hung onto every word she was saying. Could he trust Isobel enough to even try and find out how she felt about him? What if they got closer—as close as he was yearning for right now—and then she changed her mind and simply vanished from his life again? Because it wouldn't be just his life she was leaving. Oscar and Josh would be asking where she was every day. Their little hearts would be aching from missing her.

He had to protect his boys. Rafe was an adult and he could handle the fallout when a relationship of any kind failed. His sons had been too young to have been visibly traumatised by their mother's departure, but if Isobel did anything to hurt them when they were already showering her with the kind of unconditional love children were so able to give, it would be unforgivable.

'What about if we get hamburgers on the way home?' The tone of his voice was overly enthusiastic as he tried to push away an unwanted level of…what was it…*yearning*? The twins shifted their gazes for a moment and the head shakes were noticeably less emphatic this time.

'What about if we go past my old house on the way,' Isobel said, 'I can show you the tree in the garden and you can see if my bead stone string is still there?'

'*Yes...*'

Stones were being stuffed into pockets and each of Isobel's hands were firmly grasped by each twin.

'Come on...let's *go*...'

Isobel was laughing as she was dragged up the slope of the stone-covered beach. Cheddar was bouncing after the trio, barking happily, but Rafe stood still for a moment. Just watching. Feeling something squeeze so tightly in his chest that it was enough to bring that prickling sensation to the back of his eyes again.

Good grief...was the emotional rollercoaster he'd been on for weeks now ever going to slow down enough for him to get off?

Did he want to get off?

Yes. He needed solid ground beneath his feet. Time to think about the implications of what was happening. To protect his boys from any fallout.

No... The swoops of that rollercoaster might be far more uncomfortable than anything in his life had been in recent years, but the climbing sensation was...well, it was exciting, that was what it was. And he had the feeling he hadn't actually reached the highest point yet.

Rafe turned into the chilly breeze as he followed his sons back to the car. Feeling emotions this intensely was a bit like being buffeted by the fresh sea air, he decided. It might not be the most pleasant sensation, but it had an extraordinary effect of making you feel so much more alive.

Time and weather had long since eroded the integrity of the string Isobel had used but the stones were going to last for ever and all that had changed was that they were lying, half buried under plants and earth, in the garden beneath the old silver birch tree.

'Keep looking,' Isobel encouraged the twins. 'I'm sure there were more of them.' She bit her lip as she glanced up. 'Sorry—they're getting a bit dirty.'

Rafe smiled at her. 'They're six-year-old boys. Getting dirty is part of their job description.'

Oh…there was something different about that smile.

Did that have something to do with that kiss?

Isobel knew she needed to stop thinking about it because it was only making it seem more significant and she was fairly sure that that significance was very likely to be purely one-sided. She had to stop herself looking into those distorting mirrors, especially if she was going to be back in Raphael Tanner's life long-term. Not as in them getting back together. She only had to remember the expression on Rafe's face when he'd seen her arrive at the funeral to be reminded how much had changed between them. It would be a new kind of relationship, with her being an aunt to Oscar and Josh and a mother to the sister of his sons.

Now, that decision she'd made with such conviction *was* something really significant.

Totally life-changing.

Saying it out loud had made it real but hadn't diminished how right the decision felt. Rafe's approval had only made it shine a little more—brightly enough to see it as the new sun her world was going to revolve around. Instead of being scared by the prospect, however, Isobel couldn't wait to get the ball rolling to make it happen.

'I'll go and see Mum's solicitor on Monday. I have no idea how to go about starting an adoption process.'

'It'll be much easier for you than it would have been for me,' Rafe said. 'I doubt that we're ever going to find out who her father is so you're the closest relative she's got.'

'It could be possible to find him,' Isobel suggested. 'They can do astonishing things by tracing biological family through DNA now.'

'Would you want to go down that track?'

Isobel shook her head. 'If it's possible that Lauren didn't even know who the father was, it's very unlikely that he would welcome the news but it could open a whole can of worms if his relatives got involved.'

The choice to keep Daisy safe from a tug-of-war, not only between strangers but between countries, felt as right as the decision to raise her as her own child.

'If it was something that Daisy wanted to do when she's old enough, I'd support that,' Isobel added, 'but all she needs for now is to be safe. And loved. She'll have a mother. And an uncle...' Isobel had to swallow a lump that suddenly appeared in her throat. 'You're such a great dad, Rafe,' she said quietly. 'I know you'll be the best uncle.' She cleared her throat. 'And she has brothers. That pretty much adds up to a whole family, doesn't it?'

'More than I grew up with, that's for sure. And I've never been tempted to go looking for the man who fathered me. He obviously didn't want me enough to hang around.' Rafe looked as though he had a lump to swallow as well. He cleared his throat a moment later, looking away from her towards the back of the house. 'You even have a home almost ready for her, judging by the building work I could see through the windows. I'm sure that will count in your favour as well, as far as the adoption process goes.' He looked back to catch her gaze. 'I meant what I said, Belle. I'm really happy that you're so sure about this. And that you're not going to disappear again.'

And there it was again. The whisper of this being about more than adopting Daisy. It was right in front of them. That kiss…

But Isobel didn't want to talk about it. Maybe she didn't want Rafe to make the magic of those mirrors vanish for ever by admitting that he didn't quite trust her not to flee to the other side of the world again. It might not be such a good idea to keep looking into those mirrors either, but it felt like it needed to be her choice to stop and she needed a bit more time to get her head into the right space, given the emotional overload of the past weeks. Maybe she'd never really processed the heartbreak of losing the future she'd wanted so much?

Yes… She needed time. And a bit of space. Rather urgently, in fact.

'Would you mind dropping me at St Luke's before you take the boys for hamburgers? I need to visit Daisy. I can get a taxi home.'

'No problem. They'll be hanging out to get you to help make the strings, though.'

'I'll be back in time to start that before bed-time. If you've got string, that is?'

'I think there's garden twine in the shed. That natural brown sort?'

'That's perfect. Rustic is good. We can make the strings and then find driftwood later to give them something to hang from.'

'They love fossicking around in the shed so that should keep them out of mischief for a while. They'll need a good long bath to get rid of all that dirt too, so that's the rest of our afternoon sorted.'

'They can put the stones in the bath with them. And you can supervise sharing them out so I don't have to be the referee.'

Rafe laughed. 'You're not silly, are you? A

visit to Daisy will save you all that angst over who gets which stones. I promise they'll be in their PJs and guarding their personal stone piles by the time you get home.'

The sense of being given a reprieve made Isobel smile. Okay, they were going to have to talk about that kiss some time but not immediately. Maybe never, in fact, if she was right that it didn't mean anything significant to Rafe, so it would be wise to leave it up to him to broach the subject. Maybe he'd meant to kiss her cheek but she'd just moved her head or something. Whatever. If it meant nothing, they could both pretend it hadn't happened and, eventually, she could just forget about it.

Yeah…right…

CHAPTER NINE

IT FELT DIFFERENT.

From the moment Isobel walked back into the house that evening, Rafe could sense the difference.

'How's Daisy?'

'Hmm…' Isobel was taking off her coat. 'She seems okay but she didn't want her bottle. And she wouldn't settle to sleep in kangaroo care. It was like something wasn't quite right.'

Rafe was feeling that way himself. He couldn't quite put his finger on what it was, but it was definitely a hint of something awkward. Confusing, anyway.

Like the echoes of that kiss? Or was it the glimmer of something being uncovered enough to be seen again—like the shimmer of an unexpectedly different future? Judging by the way Isobel avoided direct eye contact by heading to where the twins were sitting in front of the fire playing with their stones, she was feeling it too. Talking about it wasn't likely to be easy but Rafe knew it would only get harder the longer it was left. And if they left it too long it might get shoved into a 'too hard' box and become another part of the past that they couldn't talk about. He didn't want that to happen. He wanted something new between himself and Isobel. Something real and honest, even if the prospect was daunting. He needed to know where he stood so that he could be confident that his boys were safe.

'Fancy a glass of wine?'

'Yes…please.' Isobel had discarded her coat and bag and was already on the rug beside the twins.

'Daddy's been telling us stories. About the stones,' Josh told her.

'Ledges.' Oscar nodded.

'Legends.' Rafe handed Isobel the glass of wine and then sat on the couch. 'Turns out there's quite a lot to find out about hag stones. Also known as adder stones, apparently. Or witch stones. Held in high regard by the Druids.'

Josh handed Isobel a ball of twine. 'We found the string. In the shed.'

'And spiders. There were lots of spiders.' Oscar's eyes were wide. 'I don't like spiders.'

'Don't tell anyone…' Isobel leaned close to him and spoke in a stage whisper that made Oscar giggle. 'But I don't like spiders either. They're really scary.'

'Not as scary as snakes,' Josh said. 'Daddy says the snakes all got together and used their poison to make the holes in the stones.'

'We did look at some natural causes,' Rafe put in. 'Like the holes being created by small shellfish, or water movement. Not quite as exciting as snake venom, I guess.'

'I guess not.'

'And one legend has it that if you close one eye and look through the hole in the stone, you can see a magical world.'

'Oh… I like that one.' Isobel picked up a stone and held it to her eye.

'What can you see, Aunty Belle?'

'Ooh…' Isobel turned her head, scanning the room and then her smile widened. 'I can see Daddy.'

The boys laughed. 'That's not magic,' Josh declared.

It kind of was, as far as Rafe was concerned. He could actually *feel* that smile rather than simply seeing it. He might be on the wrong side of that hole, but he could feel a bit of magic going on, himself. He took a long sip of his wine. Yep. They were going to have to talk about this. Preferably as soon as the boys were in bed. He had to know how Isobel felt about it because…she didn't look as if she was upset about anything. Quite the opposite…

Being a Saturday, with extra time allowed up, getting the children to bed took long enough for Rafe to finish his glass of wine and pour another one. Isobel helped them thread twine through the holes in the stones and tie knots to hold them in place.

'Bedtime in five minutes,' Rafe finally warned.

'No…we're not finished.'

'But it's a good time to stop,' Isobel said. 'Because you can have a think about whether you want one long string or a few short strings. When we find a nice piece of driftwood we can tie the strings onto it and then hang them somewhere. In your room, maybe? Or outside, on a tree?'

'When can we find the driftwood?'

'You'll have to ask Daddy.'

'Daddy? Can we go to the beach again tomorrow? *Please?*'

'How 'bout you see how fast you can get yourselves into bed and asleep and if it's really, really fast then I reckon we could go to the beach again tomorrow.'

'Will you come too, Aunty Belle?'

'Not this time, sweetheart. I'm going to spend tomorrow with Daisy. She wasn't so happy today and I think she might need more cuddles.'

Oscar put his arms around Isobel's neck. 'I need a cuddle.'

Josh was on her other side. 'Me too. Will you come and tuck us in, Aunty Belle?'

'Only if you guys stop strangling me.' But Isobel was laughing. 'I can't move.'

Isobel could feel it the moment she walked back into the living room, having left two very sleepy boys snuggled under their matching duvets.

It was still there, as if it had only happened a heartbeat ago.

That kiss…

And it felt as if she was standing at a cross-roads where she had to choose the direction she would take towards her future, but that was something she had already done today when she knew that she had to adopt her baby niece. It was too much to have to make another huge decision so soon but it couldn't simply be left to evaporate—or not—on its own because it had changed something.

It had opened a door to the past that was not going to quietly swing shut again.

Rafe had topped up her glass of wine while she'd been tucking the boys in to bed.

'Just a nightcap,' he said. 'It's been quite a day, hasn't it?'

'Mmm.' It still was. Isobel sat in the armchair at right angles to the couch, which put her close to Rafe but with a gap between them. A safety barrier?

He raised his glass. 'You're going to be the best mum,' he said quietly. 'My boys absolutely adore you.'

'The feeling's mutual.' Isobel touched her glass against his. 'I'm just sad about how much of their lives I've missed already.'

'Yeah...' She heard the slow breath that Rafe pulled in. 'But at least you were a mysterious person who lived on the other side of the world. It was worse that their own mother didn't want to be part of their lives. Or their grandmother. It was well beyond sad. I've been angry about it for the longest time and… and when I saw you arrive at the funeral it felt like that anger was never going to go away. It actually went up a notch or two.'

Isobel nodded slowly. 'I know. I knew how angry you were and you had every right to be. I'm…sorry…'

'No. I'm the one who should apologise. It was all my fault, after all.'

Isobel couldn't meet his gaze. She'd always believed that herself, hadn't she? So why did it feel more and more as if Rafe shouldn't be taking all the blame? She opened her mouth to tell him how her perspective had changed but he was talking again.

'How much do you know about my marriage?' His breath came out in a huff of unamused laughter. 'My *first* marriage, that is. We never really talked about it, did we?'

'Apart from you saying you were never, ever going to do it again?' Isobel shrugged. 'It didn't seem relevant. It was in the past. I figured you'd talk about it one day if you wanted to but it didn't matter if you didn't. I'm not one to base my opinions of people on gossip.'

'I didn't talk about it to anyone,' Rafe said. 'Because I didn't want to. And probably because it made me look like an idiot. When the marriage finally imploded it turned out that everybody knew about the affair except me. My wife's lover was in and out of the ED all the time on cardiology consults and I had no idea at all.' Rafe paused long enough to swallow, looking down at his hands. 'We probably got married far too young,' he added quietly. 'But I was in love with her. I trusted her. I thought we had a lifetime to be together and raise a family and I could be the kind of dad that I'd never had and always wanted so much. All those dreams and that trust got shattered in fairly spectacular fashion and it was painful enough to make sure I was never going to let it happen again. There was never any chance of it happening again.' He raised his gaze to catch Isobel's. 'Until I met you.'

Isobel caught her breath. So he had been thinking that he might want to marry her and raise a family with her? Had they been on the cusp of sharing the same dreams? Had she messed it up by revealing too much of how she felt, too soon?

'I was too obvious, wasn't I?' she said aloud. 'You must have known how much I was in love with you. And how much I was hoping you'd change your mind about getting married again. I scared you off…'

'I scared myself off,' Rafe said. 'As soon as I realised that I was falling in love with *you*. And then, when I broke it off, I realised how much I was missing you. I only went to that Christmas party because I thought you'd be there. The only thing I wanted was for us to be together again. But you weren't there. And someone came up and introduced herself as your sister and she told me where you were and…and I should have known she was lying but…she made it sound like everybody except me knew about you and Michael and…'

'And it was history repeating itself,' Isobel finished for him. 'It was a perfect storm really, because it was history repeating itself for me as well.'

The frown lines on Rafe's forehead were puzzled.

'I'd been competing with Lauren ever since she was born,' Isobel told him. 'And I always came second. Always… When I met you, I think it was the first time I ever felt like I was being chosen. That I wasn't second best.' Isobel let her breath out in a sigh. 'That's why I'd never introduced you to my family. I didn't really want you to meet Lauren.'

There was a long beat of silence.

'I'm sorry.' Rafe closed his eyes as if his thoughts hurt. 'Like I said…my fault.'

'Nothing's that black and white,' Isobel said. 'Like any disaster, there are links in the chain and taking any one of them out could have changed everything. Technically, we weren't together so I shouldn't have reacted as if you were cheating on me. That kind of makes it Lauren's fault because she knew how devastated I was. I suspect she knew I was only going to that party to see you again.'

'And, even if it had been true that you and Michael *had* hooked up, I had no right to feel like *you* were cheating on *me*. Especially seeing as I was the one who broke us up.' He offered her a wry smile. 'The grapevine at St Luke's was on your side, if it's any comfort. Especially after Lauren left me. Two wives had run off with other men. "No smoke without fire" was the general impression—I was clearly bad husband material.'

Isobel shook her head. 'I hope you don't actually believe that.'

'But it's true.' Rafe drank the last of his wine. 'I was too young the first time round, and my career was the most important thing in my life. With the long shifts and extra study, we barely saw each other. She needed something I wasn't giving her. And I was never in love with Lauren, but the boys became the most important thing ever. They still are.'

Isobel met his gaze. 'I get that,' she said softly. She picked up her glass to finish her own wine because this felt like a punctuation point. A pause, because a decision was about to be made. 'Daisy has to be the most important thing in my life from now on. What she needs feels more important than what I want.'

And there it was. The choice of direction. One road had Isobel's life—her heart and soul—firmly focused on the tiny baby she'd fallen so totally in love with. The other made Rafe just as important. Possibly more important because it was still there.

It wasn't that kiss that was still there this time, however.

It was that feeling. The one Isobel had been aware of when she'd first met Rafe. The knowing that Rafe had been the person she had found without realising that she'd been searching for him. The person that she'd wanted to spend her life with. The man she loved.

She took a deep breath. This was the most honest conversation they'd ever had and, way more than living in the same house or starting to work together, this felt like a completely fresh start.

She smiled at Rafe. 'It doesn't mean we can't be...you know...'

What had she been going to say before something stopped her? That what she wanted the most might be exactly what Daisy needed the most? That she and Rafe could be together? Be open to falling in love all over again? Be a real family?

'Be friends...?' Rafe supplied. 'The best of friends?'

'Mmm...' The sound was somewhat strangled.

Putting the children first didn't mean that

Isobel didn't want him to kiss her again. *Really* kiss her this time, even knowing where it was highly likely to lead. But how could she suggest that they could be physically close and still protect the children? Or admit to how much she'd been thinking about how amazing the sex had always been with Rafe. How badly she wanted to do more than simply relive the echoes?

It wasn't so much the thought of scaring him off again. It was more that there was nothing needy or desperate about Isobel Matthews these days. She wasn't likely to run away and hide if something went wrong either, but Rafe might need time to trust that history wasn't going to repeat itself yet again. She hadn't given him enough time at the beginning, but it was something she could do now.

She stopped herself saying anything at all.

It turned out that it was a bit harder to be the one to end that eye contact, though.

Dear Lord… The way Isobel was *looking* at him.

He'd seen that look before. That invitation. He knew the steps to this dance too. The kissing. The touches. The way everything else became so totally irrelevant because every single one of his senses was drowning in overwhelming pleasure. The sight and scents of her body, the tiny sounds of both desire and satisfaction that she would make, the way it felt to touch her and *be* touched by her. The *taste* of her...

He couldn't look away. The part of his brain that was sounding an alarm was being instantaneously silenced by another part. An entire argument in the space of only a few heartbeats.

The boys are in the house.

They're asleep. I'll hear them if they wake up. If they come looking for me, they'll go to my room, not the guest suite. They won't know...

You've just said that they're the most important thing in your life.

They are! But that doesn't mean I can never do something for myself. Something that I want. Something I think I might desperately need.

But...

It doesn't mean that I'm putting the boys at risk. We're both adults. We're both going

*to put our children first. I know I can trust
Belle. I should have always trusted her. And
she wants this as much as I do...*

That did it. Stifled the sound of the alarm
enough for Rafe to reach out and take the
wine glass from Isobel's unresisting fingers
and put it down on the coffee table without
breaking the gaze that was still locked on her
eyes. He could even remember the very first
step of that dance, when the invitation was
accepted and he steadied her chin with the
pad of his thumb. As if he needed to know
exactly where to find her lips as he closed his
eyes, tilting his head as he bent towards her.

Isobel automatically closed her eyes as she felt
the touch of his thumb under her chin, as if
her body knew exactly what she needed to do
to make the most of this moment. This way,
she could really feel the warmth of Rafe's
skin and breath as he moved closer. She could
smell the wine and another, deliciously mas-
culine scent that she had forgotten until it
filled her nostrils again—the scent that was
purely Rafe's and was only noticeable when
you were *this* close. When it wasn't going to

be swept away by a sea breeze or so brief it almost didn't happen.

Isobel could delight in the sensation that rocked her all the way to her toes at the first touch of his lips. She felt her head tipping back as her lips parted to beg for this kiss to be deepened. This would have been unthinkable for a first kiss in a new relationship but this sensation was also deep in her cell memory and she wanted the magic she knew he'd make with both his lips and his tongue. She knew that, in another heartbeat, he would be sliding his fingers into her hair…like *that*… and the press of his fingertips would be as arousing as this kiss.

It would be incredibly hard to turn off the desire that was rapidly escalating out of control but Isobel had to give Rafe that option when they finally ended this kiss. What if he'd just been responding to what he must have seen in her eyes? She'd know for sure, as soon as she caught his gaze again, whether he wanted this as much as she did. She'd also know whether it was pushing boundaries too far for anything to happen in the house his sons were sleeping in.

She did know—the moment his gaze caught

hers again—because that intense focus of those dark, dark eyes unlocked another memory. The one where *she* was the most important person on earth to Rafe and she felt exactly the same way about him. Where, for the length of time it took for a physical conversation to celebrate that, the rest of the world was irrelevant.

'Come with me.' His voice was almost a growl.

They couldn't get down the hallway fast enough but Rafe paused for as long as it took to peep into the boys' room and check that they were sound asleep. He closed the door of their room quietly. Moments later, he closed the door of Isobel's room behind them just as quietly.

It felt like another tiny pause. It could have been long enough for either one of them to change their mind but it did the complete opposite. Isobel could feel the flames of desire become white hot and the heat seemed to be contagious because Rafe was unbuttoning his shirt to pull it off and then reaching to help Isobel take off her jersey and the tee shirt she was wearing beneath it. The garments puddled on the floor beside them and then there was another pause. A moment of palpable stillness as they stood there, simply looking at each other.

Had Isobel forgotten how beautiful Rafe's body was, or was the real thing simply so much more intense than a memory? His gorgeous olive brown skin and the irresistible copper disks of his nipples. Oh…and that soft arrow of dark hair that dragged her gaze down to the waistband of his jeans. She *had* forgotten what it felt like to release the stud button on his jeans. And the way the rasp of a zip opening could make it unbearable to wait any longer, but she remembered how Rafe would make her wait, teasing her with his hands and lips and tongue until she was begging him to give her what she needed the most.

And that wait would end up being the best part because it made her feel as if *she* was worth waiting for.

She hoped he would still whisper her name when he reached his own peak. It was on his lips now as his hands reached to trace the shape of her breasts before undoing her bra.

'Belle…'

CHAPTER TEN

THIS FELT LIKE a genuinely clean slate.

Okay, you could see old writing that could never be completely wiped clean, but that was all it was. Something that had happened that couldn't be changed. Ghosts from the past that would always be there if you went looking for them. Unfortunate things had happened, like the aftermath of that Christmas party and the lack of loyalty from Isobel's family that had led to its disintegration, but there had been unknown, complicating factors on both sides that had played a big part and knowledge could lead to both understanding and forgiveness.

Tragic things had more recently been layered on top of what had happened so long ago, with the deaths of Lauren and Sharon Matthews and the birth of orphaned Daisy but, with everything out in the open between herself and Rafe, and the benefit of distance in time, Isobel could clearly see that it was not the total fault of any particular person involved. They were all to blame in some ways but the tragic finality that had brought her back into Rafe's life meant that everything that had come before was now irrelevant.

That first stolen night together was not only the start of something new and wonderful. It was the beginning of something even better than it had ever been. Life itself seemed better than it had ever been as the busy days slipped past, full of work and children and hospital visits, a house that was dry enough for the rebuilding to be well underway, wheels in motion for Daisy's adoption and steps in place to break the lease on Isobel's apartment in New Zealand and ship her personal items back to England.

Everything was perfect.

Except that Daisy wasn't well again.

The tiny baby had been a little out of sorts the day of the bead stone collecting and she had been running a slight temperature the next day, when Rafe took the twins back to the beach to hunt for some driftwood branches, but every parent in NICU knew to expect that their time in the intensive care unit was unlikely to progress completely smoothly. Most described it as a rollercoaster where it felt as if you were taking three steps forwards and then two backwards. There were always setbacks, sometimes small, sometimes large and, sadly, sometimes life-threatening.

That first setback for Daisy had only been small and she had recovered within a couple of days so Isobel was hopeful that whatever was causing Daisy to be irritable and unhappy again only a week later would be resolved just as easily. Isobel spent the entire day in the NICU that Sunday and managed to coax Daisy into drinking a little milk and she had been more than happy to remain in the armchair with skin-to-skin contact with the fragile infant for as long as Daisy was content.

Isobel talked to her softly as she fell asleep and didn't move after those dark eyes stopped staring into her own and drifted shut as one hour ticked over into another. Private words that were no more than whispered promises.

'Tomorrow, I'm going to talk to the solicitor about the next steps in adopting you, little one. There'll be lots of other people to talk to as well, I expect, and hundreds of pieces of paper to sign but, by the time you're big and strong enough to come home, you'll be my little girl. It'll be you and me in our own house.'

Daisy's head was still so small it fitted too easily into the cradle of Isobel's cupped hand.

'There's a tree in the back yard and we'll put a swing out there. We'll go to the beach too, when you're a bit bigger, and find the stones with the holes in them to make a string that's just for you. I'll tell you how you can close one eye and look through the hole and see a magical place.'

Isobel had looked through the hole in one of the bead stones and she'd seen Rafe...

It might be more complicated to find a way to steal more of those magic nights together, but it might also be a good thing. Rafe had said that it wasn't until he'd broken off their initial relationship that he'd realised how much he was missing her. Living in a different house might make him realise how much they all needed to be together. And, if real magic happened and he found himself falling in love with her all over again, they could all be together. As a real family.

'You've got the best uncle anyone could

ever have, my love. And two big brothers. They'll all be there to look after you whenever you need them.'

Isobel certainly wasn't going to jump the gun in any way because this new honesty and deeper level of trust between herself and Rafe was something too precious to risk breaking so it didn't matter how long it took. Even if it never changed from what it was right now, it was a broken dream that was, amazingly, being glued back to almost its original shape. And there was so much to look forward to.

'I'm going to choose the colours for your bedroom this week, darling. Not pink, though, and no unicorns. Shall we go for yellow and blue? Like a summer sky and sunshine? Maybe some soft green somewhere, like grass, and I could paint daisies everywhere. Daisies for Daisy...'

An alarm began to sound and a nurse was swiftly by Isobel's side.

'Did you forget to breathe for a second, button?' The nurse tapped Daisy's foot gently to stimulate a response and they could both see the tiny chest expand. 'What's going on? You haven't had one of those for a long time.' Her tone, as she gathered the baby into her hands, was a lot calmer than Isobel felt. 'Let's put her back in her incubator. Just to make sure we've got everything monitored properly.'

Isobel could still sit with her and help with her care, like changing her nappy, but Daisy was still miserable and by late that afternoon, after another apnoeic episode, a NICU consultant and her team were called in to assess her.

'It looks like it might be the first signs of an infection,' she told Isobel. 'But try not to worry too much. We're going to get on top of this as fast as we can.'

The specialist turned to the group of staff around her and, despite being a medical professional herself—or perhaps because she understood too much of what was being left unsaid, Isobel found her head spinning as she listened to a discussion around her that was full of potential dangers to this tiny baby beside her.

Her baby.

It was impossible not to worry too much. Antibiotics were being charted. Blood tests ordered. Forms for blood cultures being signed. Urine cultures and chest X-rays were discussed. A lumbar puncture was also mentioned and it was at that point that worry tipped into fear for Isobel. She knew why a lumbar puncture might be required and she knew all too well how dangerous an infection like meningitis could be to any baby, let alone one that still hadn't reached the weight and stage of development of an average newborn.

There was nothing Isobel could do for Daisy. She couldn't even be close enough to the incubator now, to talk to Daisy or put her hand through an access port and touch a tiny foot or cradle her head. All too soon there were doctors, nurses and technicians crowded into the space, more medical equipment with monitors and trolleys going in and out, and sometimes Isobel could only catch a glimpse of a small brown bear that had become wedged between the mattress inside the incubator and the plastic wall at the end.

Some of the specialist staff hadn't met Isobel before and maybe they didn't know her story.

'The best thing you can do, Mum, is to go home for a while and get some rest yourself. We'll have a better idea of what we're dealing with tomorrow and, in the meantime, if anything changes we'll call you straight away.'

It didn't feel at all weird for someone to assume she was Daisy's mother because, in the space of just a few short weeks, that was how Isobel was feeling about this baby. Looking back, that rush of overwhelming love and the need to protect this child had probably come, without any warning, with that first touch. When she'd reached into the incubator to put her fingertip on Daisy's palm and felt those teeny, tiny fingers closing around it.

She *was* Daisy's mother.

But there was nothing she could do to protect her and walking away that evening was the hardest thing Isobel had ever done. As the double doors into the NICU suite swung shut behind her, however, Isobel realised that she was walking in the right direction. She knew perfectly well that, in order to be strong for Daisy, she needed to try and take care of herself. She needed to go home, not just to sleep but for something she needed even more urgently.

She needed to be with Rafe.

She knew he would talk to her and offer reassurance and support on both a medical and personal level, but all she really needed in this moment was simply to be *with* him.

* * *

One look at Isobel's face when she came through the door that evening and Rafe forgot about sorting the boys' lunchboxes and backpacks for school tomorrow. He dropped homework books on the kitchen table and had Isobel in his arms before she had time to take her coat off.

'What's happened?'

'Daisy's sick… They think she's got an infection and…and maybe it's something I did? But I washed that little bear so carefully, and I always wear a gown and a mask, and I've never sanitised my hands so often in my life and…and…'

Apart from the day of the funeral, when it was only to be expected, the last time Rafe had seen Isobel really fighting tears had been in this kitchen, that night she'd arrived home late with the odd little brown bear in her bag, although she'd come close that first day of doing kangaroo care with Daisy, judging by the sparkle in her eyes. And Rafe was pretty sure he'd tasted tears when he'd kissed her on the beach that day but he hadn't been entirely sure that those tears weren't his own. This time was very different. These weren't tears that had any element of happiness or poignancy or even grief mixed into their cause. This was deep misery.

Fear…

'And…oh, Rafe… I don't know what to do and I'm really, really scared.'

Isobel buried her face against his chest as she burst into tears and Rafe could swear he felt something crack in his own heart at the sound of her sobbing. As he tightened his hold and bent his head to press his cheek against her hair, all he could think was how much he wished he could take this pain and fear away from her and shoulder it himself.

And then he realised that you only ever felt like that about someone you truly loved and that stole his breath away completely.

He'd been *in* love with this woman long ago, with all the overwhelming emotions that went with that—and all the pain that came from losing it. He'd been so badly hurt by her and angry with her for such a long time but more recently he'd been impressed by her all over again and…yeah…attracted to her all over again as well. He hadn't forgotten how astonishingly good the sex had always been between them but he had been amazed to discover it seemed to be even better the second time around.

He understood her far better than he ever had too—how had he not known that she'd lived in her sister's shadow all her life? And they had a new bond in the way they felt as parents, because there was no doubt that Isobel had become Daisy's parent and he knew only too well how huge that was.

But the way he was feeling right now, as he held Isobel until she'd released enough of her own emotions to be able to talk to him, was something different. Something that was a combination of everything else and more. Something deeper than anything else.

Soul deep.

The kind of love that had actually been there all along, possibly from the moment he'd met Isobel.

The kind of love that could last a lifetime.

'Come and sit down,' he said gently, guiding her towards a chair with his hands on her shoulders. 'And tell me everything that's happening.'

Rafe had been able to offer real comfort when Isobel had been overwhelmed by the new direction her life was taking, by telling her that she didn't need to know what to do, she just needed to keep doing what she *was* doing and take one day at a time.

What was happening now, with this crisis for Daisy, meant that there was no way she *could* do anything, but the underlying message of taking one day at a time was still helpful. And this time there was more that Rafe could do to support Isobel when it became apparent by the next day that the worst was yet to come. Baby Daisy had pneumonia.

Rafe could—and did—take away any obligation for Isobel to be anywhere other than in NICU during the day by finding a new agency who were able to provide a locum practice nurse. He could—and did—make time to be there at St Luke's with her as often as possible. Helen was more than happy to spend more hours looking after the house and the twins. The staff at the Harrison Street Medical Centre knew Isobel now and were only too willing to offer whatever assistance they could and when Oscar and Josh told their friends that their baby sister was very sick, other parents began to step in to help as well.

It felt, to Isobel, as if she'd not only found

the closest thing to a real family by coming back to Balclutha. She'd found an entire village. She drew strength from that support as she watched Daisy become even more unwell over the next few days. There was no kangaroo care now. She was back on CPAP, which meant her button of a nose was covered by a snugly fitting mask on the end of a tube, attached to equipment which delivered air at a constant pressure to keep air sacs open and prevent apnoeic episodes. The function of every major organ in that tiny body was being carefully watched, by monitors and electrodes and blood tests amongst the battery of technology and expertise that was available.

Rafe was in NICU with Isobel the afternoon that Daisy's team decided they needed to gain peripheral arterial access to monitor both her blood pressure levels as accurately as possible and her blood gas levels to see how much oxygen was circulating and how much carbon dioxide was being removed by her lungs. She knew this was an invasive enough procedure to be a warning that they were still a long way from getting on top of this crisis. And it was terrifying.

It felt as if it could be the beginning of the end.

And Isobel's heart was breaking. Because she knew she had found what she wanted most in her life- -a family of her own— and she was in very real danger of having it simply ripped away from her if this baby she loved so much couldn't survive this. She didn't want to go back to her old life. She couldn't. What she had found here with Daisy and Oscar and Josh and Rafe was so different she could look back on her life in New Zealand and realise that, while it might have been professionally the best it could have been, it had been missing something far more important.

Love. People to care about and *be* cared about by. She couldn't go back to the loneliness that she'd sadly become so used to. She *wouldn't* go back but, if she lost Daisy, she would lose the foundation stone of the new life she wanted more than anything.

In this moment, she knew that Rafe was another foundation stone. He was probably losing all feeling in his hand with her clutching it so tightly, but he wasn't showing any sign of discomfort. He stood by her side when Isobel refused to leave Daisy alone with her medical team—a solid human rock rather than a simple stone, that she could cling to as tightly as necessary. Far enough away for any whispered conversation not to disturb what was happening.

Isobel watched as Daisy's wrist was pressed by fingers that looked large enough to be hurting her and squeezed Rafe's hand even more tightly. 'What are they doing?'

'It's called an Allen's test,' Rafe told her. 'You block both the radial and ulnar arteries in the wrist and then release the ulnar. If normal colour returns fast enough then the collateral circulation is okay and the radial artery can be cannulated.'

Maybe it would be easier to focus on something clinical, Isobel decided. But looking at what was being arranged on the sterile drape didn't help. There was antiseptic, and a cannula with its hollow needle that might be the smallest size available but it still looked far too big for Daisy's arm. She could see syringes and an infusion bag for flushing the lines, a three-way tap that would be used to withdraw blood for testing and transducers and cables that would be monitoring blood pressure. And there was more tubing and wires to add to what Daisy had already collected in the last few days.

Isobel closed her eyes tightly. Best not to look. Best just to hold Rafe's hand.

'It's not hurting her.' Rafe had bent his head so that he could whisper right beside her ear. 'She's fast asleep with the sedation she's been given.' His lips were close enough to tickle. 'Deep breath, hon. Daisy might know that you're here and she needs her mum to be strong.'

Isobel leaned into the warmth of his voice and the feel of his hand enclosing her own. She kept her eyes closed and just held on physically and let go mentally, deliberately not thinking about what was happening here. In the next few minutes, until the procedure was over, thoughts bubbled to the surface and then drifted away to allow others to take their place. There was grief there for her sister and mother. Fear for Daisy but also a wash of love that was so powerful Isobel knew it had changed her for ever. And there was also the realisation that her love for this man, standing beside her and holding her up, was just as powerful.

This wasn't a dream of what a perfect future could look like. Or a peek into a distorted mirror. This had no connection to the future. Or the past, for that matter—even the most recent past that included their lovemaking—because, in this moment, both the future and past were irrelevant. This awareness was so all-encompassing that her mind, and heart, could only soak in this moment. Her love for Raphael Tanner was simply there. A fact of life, as much as the way her heart was beating without needing any conscious direction. As solid as the man himself and as real as the grip of his hand around her own.

Isobel opened her eyes and took in a slow, deep breath. She could do this. She could be strong for Daisy and cope with whatever was going to come, as long as she had Rafe by her side.

CHAPTER ELEVEN

RAFE'S HEART WAS BREAKING. Both for baby Daisy and for Isobel. The procedure to insert an arterial line had been so hard to watch that it was probably just as well that Isobel wasn't there in the middle of the night a couple of days later when the team made the decision to intubate this tiny baby because the levels of carbon dioxide still in her blood were dangerously high and she needed more help to breathe. Isobel had finally been persuaded to come home for a few hours to get the kind of sleep that was impossible when she was in the armchair beside Daisy's incubator.

The chair where Rafe had first seen her holding Daisy with that oh, so small head nestled between her breasts and he'd seen—and remembered—exactly why he'd fallen in love with this woman. It was nearly a week since Daisy had become so sick and days since she'd even opened her eyes. There was talk about multi-organ failure, so antibiotics and other drugs were being carefully juggled.

They needed a miracle, but when it began to happen it seemed too rapid to be trustworthy. How could blood gas levels return to being within normal parameters so quickly after the addition of extra assistance from a ventilator? Vital signs like blood pressure and heart rate were stabilising and the function of organs like her kidneys were heading towards acceptable levels. One by one, the tubes and wires and monitoring equipment were being taken away.

The next time Rafe stole some time from work to visit, he had fully expected to find Isobel sitting in that familiar armchair in NCIU but the last thing he'd expected to find was that she had the baby—*her* baby—snuggled against her skin again.

'It's just for a short time today.' Isobel's voice wobbled. 'But she's doing so well, they thought she deserved a cuddle. She's lost weight but it really looks like she's finally beaten this infection.'

Rafe didn't care that he had tears rolling down his face as he crouched beside the chair to gaze at Daisy's little face, fast asleep and utterly content.

'She's a wee fighter,' he said softly. 'She wants to be here, that's for sure.'

'I want her to be here,' Isobel whispered. 'More than I could ever have imagined. It's weird, isn't it?'

'What?'

'That she's only been in my life for such a short time but I can't imagine my life without her.'

'That's how fast it can happen.' Rafe smiled as he nodded his complete understanding. 'I felt like that the first moment I held Oscar and Josh.'

Isobel wiped away a tear. 'How are the boys? I feel like I've barely seen them for far too long.'

'They're good. They'll be so happy to know that their little sister is getting better. Even happier, though, I have to admit, that they're going to their friend Simon's birthday party and sleepover tonight. It's a pirate party and there's even going to be a boat that arrives on a trailer and there's some mechanism that means it can be rocked like they're sailing through a stormy sea.' He glanced up at a large clock on the wall. 'I can't stay too long because I promised I'd be back in time after school to help them get dressed up. We've got costumes with eye patches and hats and swords and everything.'

'I'm sorry I won't see them.'

'I'll take lots of photos,' Rafe promised. 'And I'm going to cook something special for us too. We can have our own party to celebrate this little miracle...' He used the tip of his forefinger to stroke Daisy's cheek. A featherlike touch that was intended not to wake her up but she felt it. Her face scrunched up and then relaxed again, except for one side of her mouth that was still curled up.

'Oh, my God...' Rafe breathed. 'Is she *smiling*?'

'She heard you calling her a little miracle,' Isobel whispered. 'I think she liked that.'

It might have only been a small curl of Daisy's lips but it had wrapped itself entirely around Rafe's heart. He was feeling a bond with this baby that was right up there with how he felt about his own boys and the ripple of that bone-deep emotion was including the woman who was holding this precious infant.

It was not the first time he'd felt the need to

care for and protect Isobel, but it was getting stronger every time. And, man, she needed a bit of pampering after the rough week she'd just been through. It looked as if it hadn't been only Daisy who'd lost weight and those dark shadows under Isobel's eyes were all too obvious against her paler than usual skin. He found himself trying to remember something that he knew would make her happy.

'Is Mexican food still your most favourite thing in the world to eat?'

Isobel blinked. 'I can't believe you remembered that. Yes, I still love it.'

'Tacos?'

'And nachos. And quesadillas.' Isobel was smiling. 'I'm hungry already.'

'I'm not sure I'm up to cooking them, but I'll give it a go.'

'Don't cook.' Isobel shook her head. 'You've missed nearly as much sleep as I have in the last few days and I know how tired you must be. I'll pick up takeout on my way home.'

Home…

He knew perfectly well that Isobel and Daisy would be moving to their own home in the not-too-distant future, but life at the moment, especially while Daisy had been so sick, had become just a day at a time so it didn't matter that it felt so right to hear her say that. She *was* going to be coming home.

And the idea of her moving out to a home of her own was giving Rafe an odd empty feeling in his gut—as if he was missing her already.

The way he had when he'd backed out of their relationship all those years ago and pushed her out of his life? He didn't want to feel like that again. He wanted what they had so unexpectedly found together again and this time he wasn't about to panic. He knew he could trust this. And trust Isobel.

He'd never told her he loved her. Not directly, anyway. He'd only said that she'd been the one he'd loved rather than her sister. Past tense. Isobel had never said it to him either, even back when it was so obvious she was in love with him. Had she just been waiting for him to say the 'L' word first? Confident that it would happen, despite him telling her that he would never go there again, because what they had together was so amazing?

It *had* been amazing.

But this second time around it was even more amazing, wasn't it? More real, perhaps, because they knew each other so much more intimately. And because there were children and a baby involved who all needed their protection and love. More trustworthy, because they'd both been battered by life but what was holding them so close seemed to be growing steadily stronger.

Rafe had really given up on even the idea of marriage after Lauren had left him. He'd given up on ever trying to find love again but, just like the first time he'd had his convictions challenged, things were changing because he'd met Isobel.

Because she'd come back into his life.

It felt like time to tell her that.

But not here. There was a much better place for something so personal and private.

'Compromise,' he said, his voice slightly raw. 'You're even more exhausted than I am. Just come home and we'll get it delivered.'

It was a Mexican feast, covering the table in Isobel's favourite room of Rafe's house. They weren't sitting at the dining table because it was the old wooden work table that had become *their* place to be together, sitting at right angles to each other at the end of the table, sharing food or wine under the watchful eye of Cheddar, usually lying in *his* special place on the old couch.

This was where Isobel and Rafe had talked properly for the first time since their relationship had broken up. Where she'd learned that he'd given up a career in Emergency that he'd been so passionate about to become a GP and raise his sons. She'd learned that, shockingly, Lauren had been well advanced in a pregnancy when she'd died and that, miraculously, that baby—*her* niece—had survived.

It had been in this room that she'd first met her nephews and felt those first powerful connections that could come from the kind of unconditional acceptance and love a true family could provide. And it had also been in this room that Rafe had told her that he hadn't wanted to marry her sister. That Isobel had been the one he'd loved.

She'd found employment in a new job sitting at this table, along with the fresh start that a professional relationship promised to offer them both and that had been worthy of celebrating but this was the first time it felt as if they were having a party in this kitchen that was the heart of Rafe's house.

There were all of Isobel's favourite Mexican dishes here. A nachos platter with a nest of corn chips holding a delicious dip of refried beans, guacamole and sour cream. Crunchy fried tortillas filled with melted cheese that were the best kind of quesadillas and tacos with melt-in-the-mouth pulled beef, spicy salsa and crisp lettuce. The restaurant had also supplied the icy cold lager they were drinking with a wedge of lime stuffed into the neck of the bottles.

'There's no way we can ever eat all this food, Rafe.'

'Just as well our boys love Mexican food almost as much as you do, then.'

Our boys?

Isobel needed a moment to absorb that. Or maybe it was more that she wanted to tuck away the fact that it didn't feel odd to hear Rafe say that. That she really did feel like part of this family.

'It feels different without them here.'

'Mmm…' Rafe was smiling as he loaded another corn chip with dip. 'Quieter.'

'You know what I mean. Even when they're in bed, you know they're in the house and… and you can feel it.'

Rafe ate his chip, nodding as he swallowed. 'There speaks a true parent.' He lifted his bottle of lager, his voice softening. 'Here's to Daisy's mum for coping with a rough stretch. And here's to Daisy for being the fighter she is. May she grow up to love Mexican food as much as the rest of her family.'

'I wonder what the pirates are eating?'

'Fish fingers, I reckon.'

'Or meatballs for cannonballs?'

'Crackers. For Polly the parrot.'

'And gold coins for treasure.'

They were both laughing but not enough to account for the tears that suddenly sprang into Isobel's eyes. Rafe's smile evaporated instantly.

'What is it?' he asked quietly.

'I hope Daisy wants a pirate party one day.' Her breath hitched in a kind of hiccup. 'I was so scared she might never actually get a birthday party.'

'I know...'

Rafe took hold of Isobel's hand. His skin was chilled from where he'd been holding the cold bottle of lager and, without thinking, Isobel put her other hand on top of his.

'I've never been so scared in my life.'

'I know,' he said again.

He had put his other hand on top of Isobel's and then, in a silence that stretched on and on, their hands did a kind of slow dance—moving in and around each other, interlacing fingers with a touch that was so gentle it was astonishing that it could be felt in every cell of Isobel's body.

When she lifted her gaze it felt as if Rafe had been waiting to catch it with his own. So that she would know he was feeling it as well? The connection—and the silent communication—was so powerful there was no need for either of them to say anything out loud.

Except...there *was* a need, wasn't there?

Isobel needed to hear Rafe say it out loud. That he loved her. She needed to tell him how much she loved him out loud, not through this poignant kind of touch, however meaningful it was. She needed to tell him that she trusted him absolutely now. That she would trust him with her life in a heartbeat, because she couldn't imagine a future without him in it, any more than she could imagine one without Daisy. And she desperately needed to hear him tell her that he felt the same way.

She watched his lips part and knew he was

about to say something. Given how much love she could see in his eyes, Isobel knew that it was going to be exactly what she wanted to hear and her heart skipped a beat as she held her breath.

She was still holding her breath when Rafe's phone buzzed.

And while she watched the colour drain from his face as he listened to what sounded like a frantic female voice.

'I'm on my way,' he said, standing up as he abruptly ended the call. His eyes were so dark they looked black when he caught Isobel's gaze. 'It's Oscar,' he said. 'There's been an accident.'

It was Isobel's turn to give Rafe the kind of support he'd been giving her ever since she had crash-landed back into his life. Her training enabled her to stay calm, despite her own personal connection to this victim, in the face of what could possibly be a time-critical incident, judging by how ashen Rafe was looking.

'I'll drive.'

'I can do it.'

'I know what I'm doing, Rafe. Trust me.'

She took the keys from his hand. 'Where are we heading? Simon's house?'

'No. They called an ambulance. They're already on their way to St Luke's. Simon's mother's gone with him and she had to take Josh. I could hear him in the background.' Rafe's voice caught. 'I've never heard him sound that distraught.'

Isobel checked that Rafe had done up his safety belt and then put her foot down on the accelerator. She knew she could drive fast and keep them safe. If she got a speeding ticket, she'd deal with it later.

'What's happened to Oscar?'

'He fell from that damned boat when it was rocking. He was holding his plastic sword and it went straight into his leg on impact. It sounds like it might have hit an artery before it snapped off.'

Under Rafe's direction, Isobel parked his car in the doctors' space of the ambulance bay and when they ran into the emergency department of St Luke's Hospital they could see the stretcher holding Oscar being wheeled into one of the resuscitation rooms. A woman, presumably Simon's mother, was holding Josh, who appeared to be desperate to follow his brother and was screaming with frustration at being held back.

For a few moments, at the doors to the resuscitation room, it was fraught.

Isobel could see Oscar being transferred to the bed. A pale ghost of a little boy in a pirate's costume and face paint of a moustache and goatee beard who looked barely conscious.

She could hear the paramedics giving a swift handover.

'Heart rate of one twenty. Blood pressure seventy-six over forty.'

Isobel's heart dropped like a stone. Oscar must have lost so much blood he was in haemorrhagic shock and that was, indeed, a time-critical injury.

'Estimated blood loss approximately a litre,' the paramedic continued. 'There's no pedal pulse in the left foot.'

She could also hear Josh's sobbing as he clung to his father.

'I've got to go and look after Oscar, Josh. I'm sorry but you can't go in there.'

'*No*…don't go, Daddy. Please don't go…'

'Aunty Belle's here. She's going to look

after you.' Rafe was staring into Resus, clearly needing to see and hear what was going on.

'We couldn't get venous access,' Isobel heard a paramedic say. 'He's too shut down.'

'We'll go for central venous access for fluid resuscitation.' It looked like every ED doctor was in there with Josh and it was a senior consultant who was taking the lead. 'Type and cross-match in case we need a whole blood transfusion and get Theatre on standby.'

Rafe caught Isobel's gaze over the top of Josh's head and there was a desperate plea in his eyes.

'Come with me, sweetheart.' Isobel prised Josh away from his father and, much to her relief, he wrapped his arms around her neck and burrowed his head against her shoulder as he continued sobbing. 'Daddy's going to help look after Oscar and he'll come and tell us what's happening really soon.'

The relatives' room had a television and a DVD player. It had books and toys and snacks but there was nothing that Josh was remotely interested in. Isobel did everything she could to soothe him, holding him in her arms and rocking him as they sat on a small couch. Telling him over and over again that Oscar was being looked after by very clever doctors and nurses and they were doing everything they could to make him better. She stopped short of telling him that everything was going to be all right. She didn't know that herself so she couldn't promise something that might turn out to not be true.

It was the longest hour of her life as she waited for news. Josh eventually exhausted himself crying and fell asleep in her arms and Isobel just kept on holding him and counting every minute that ticked past. When Rafe finally came to find her, it felt as if she had frozen to the spot. She couldn't even find any words to break an awful silence as Rafe sat down on another couch and buried his face in his hands.

'He's in Theatre.' His words were muffled. 'They've repaired the artery and stopped the bleeding. They're just closing up now but he's going to be okay.'

'Oh…' Isobel had to bite her lip hard to stop herself bursting into tears which would scare Josh if he woke up. 'Thank goodness… Did he need a blood transfusion?'

'No. He responded very well to the fluid resuscitation and was stabilised enough to have a CT scan before going to Theatre, so the surgeons knew exactly what they were dealing with. I don't think the blood loss was as bad as they initially thought.'

'It's a hard thing to estimate. It can look far more than it is, especially if it's a hard surface or there's no thick clothing to soak it up.'

Rafe tipped his head back, rubbing his eyes. 'Simon's parents panicked. They knew to put pressure on a wound to stop bleeding, but they also knew not to pull out an impaled object. It wasn't till the paramedics got there and put a doughnut dressing and pressure bandage on that it was controlled at all.' He sat up. 'How's Josh been?'

'Frightened. I did my best to reassure him but I couldn't make promises that I might not have been able to keep. And… I was scared too. As scared as I was when I thought I might lose Daisy.'

Had it only been an hour or two ago that she'd been telling Rafe how terrifying that had been? When he'd held her hands and she'd been so sure he was about to tell her that he loved her? There was certainly nothing on either of their minds now other than the wellbeing of two very much-loved small boys.

'Could you take him home, Belle? So that you can both get some sleep?'

'Of course.'

'I'll carry him out to the car.'

Josh woke up as his father lifted him. 'Daddy?'

'It's okay, Josh. Everything's okay. Oscar's had an operation on his leg and it's fine. It's not bleeding any more. He needs to stay here tonight but he might be allowed to come home tomorrow.'

'Can I stay here too?'

'No. Aunty Belle is going to take you home to your own bed. I'm coming down to the car with you so I can say goodnight and then I'll stay with Oscar so he's not lonely.'

Isobel followed as he carried Josh into the corridor.

'Aunty Belle can bring you back in the morning,' Rafe told Josh as they went through ED towards the ambulance bay. 'Maybe you could bring Oscar something to wear so he doesn't need to be a pirate when we go home? You could bring him a treat for breakfast too, if you like.'

'Like a hamburger?'

Rafe chuckled. 'Sure. Why not?'

Josh was almost asleep again as he buckled him into the back seat. Rafe closed the door gently and then turned to Isobel, drawing her into his arms for a brief but fierce hug.

'I'll text you as soon as he's out of Theatre.'

Isobel hugged him back just as tightly. 'I'm with Josh. I don't want to leave you.'

'It's going to be all right.' Rafe's voice was against her ear. 'Go and get some rest, Belle.' His lips were on her temple. 'Everything's going to be all right.'

Except it wasn't.

It took only one look at Rafe's face when Isobel arrived at St Luke's with Josh the next morning to know that something was very wrong. He almost looked worse than he had last evening when he'd been about to join Oscar in the resuscitation area.

And Isobel was terrified all over again. She froze while Josh, carrying the fast-food paper bag full of treats, ran past her towards the bed he could see Oscar sitting in.

'What is it, Rafe? What's wrong?'

She took another glance towards Oscar, but he was looking far better than she'd expected this soon after his surgery. Josh was sitting on the end of the bed now and the bag was being delved into. Not for the food yet. It was the toys that had come with it that had the boys' attention first.

Rafe had followed her gaze. 'Oscar's fine,' he told her. 'He'll be discharged to go home later today after he's been seen by his surgeon.'

There was something odd about Rafe's tone. Because it lacked the joy she would have expected to hear with that news?

'I don't understand,' she said quietly. 'It's obvious that there's something wrong.'

Rafe wasn't meeting her gaze and, for some reason, that sent a chill down Isobel's spine. He'd done this once before, hadn't he? When he'd been finding the words to tell her that it was over. That he didn't want them to be together any longer. That he needed…space…

He was pulling something out of his shirt pocket. A small folded piece of paper. A test result? Isobel caught her breath. Had something shown up that was wrong with Oscar? Something serious, like leukaemia? But, if that was the case, why would Rafe have said that his son was fine?

The information on the paper made no sense either.

'This is a blood type and cross-match result,' she said. 'It's just Oscar's blood group and rhesus factor.'

Rafe's breath came out in a huff that sounded broken. 'Yeah...*just* his blood group,' he echoed.

Isobel glanced over her shoulder but the twins weren't looking at their father so they wouldn't see an expression that might have alarmed them. They were showing their toys to a nurse and eating French fries at the same time.

'Come with me,' she said to Rafe, 'and tell me what the hell's going on. Somewhere that you're not going to upset the boys.'

Rafe hesitated but then followed her, the grim expression on his face a warning that Isobel wasn't going to like what she was about to hear.

'So... Oscar's blood group is A. I don't understand what the problem is.'

'Lauren's blood was cross-matched when she came here after the accident because she *did* need a transfusion. That's how I know that her blood group was O.'

'And...?'

'So's mine. I'm an O.' Rafe shook his head

at her obvious lack of comprehension. 'It's not possible for two O parents to have an A baby,' he said slowly. 'And that means that I'm not Oscar's father. Or Josh's, obviously.'

Isobel could feel the shockwave start at the level of her ears as she heard his words but then it pulsed down, right to her feet, like a lightning bolt finding the earth.

'But that means…'

'That Lauren was already pregnant before the night of the Christmas party.' Rafe gave another one of those broken-sounding huffs of breath. 'We all thought the twins were in great shape when they were born. With better-than-expected weights. Now I know why.'

'Oh, my God…' Isobel's head was spinning. 'I had no idea. She lied to me as well. Unless…she didn't know herself? Like with Daisy?'

'She must have known there was a chance that I wasn't the father. And she definitely knew how much I loved those babies.' Rafe's voice was dangerously quiet. 'Enough to let myself get blackmailed into a marriage I never intended to have. I wasn't going to let history repeat itself and not be a father to my boys, but that wasn't difficult because I loved them.'

'I know,' Isobel whispered. She'd seen that love. That amazing bond Rafe had with the twins. He couldn't *be* a better father.

'And now it turns out that I'm not even related to them. How am I supposed to explain that? How do I tell them that their Aunty Belle is the only *real* family they've actually got? How ironic is that?' Rafe was shaking his head. 'I was worried at first that they might get hurt if they got too close to you, but the idea that our family might get destroyed never occurred to me.'

'Are you saying that this is somehow *my* fault?' The shockwave had been replaced by a numbness that was spreading just as rapidly.

Rafe turned away. 'No, I'm not saying that,' he said. 'I just wish I'd never met your sister.'

His voice was as raw as Isobel had ever heard it. So was the unspoken message. If Rafe had never met Isobel and they had never fallen in love with each other, he wouldn't have met Lauren and none of this heartbreak would have ever happened.

He might as well have said that he wished he'd never met *her*.

'Daddy?' Josh had come to the door of the paediatric surgical ward. 'Why are you out

here? We've got a hamburger for you too.'
He took hold of Rafe's hand and was pulling
him away. He looked over his shoulder as he
did so. 'There's one for you, Aunty Belle, remember?'

'Save it for me, sweetheart.' It was astonishing that Isobel could keep her tone this
cheerful and completely hide the fact that the
world felt as if it was falling away from beneath her feet. 'I'm not very hungry just at
the moment.'

Food was the last thing she wanted right
now. It was hard enough to even pull in a new
breath with this curious numbness seeping
through her body. It was a bit like that feeling when she'd first arrived back and there'd
simply been too many huge emotions to try
and process. The loss of her mother and sister.
Seeing Rafe again. The flooded house. The
news of another baby. Jetlag and exhaustion.

She needed to escape. To find somewhere
she could breathe more easily. And think. If
she could just clear the foggy feeling in her
head then perhaps she would be able to make
some sense out of what felt like a complete
disaster that she hadn't seen coming.

CHAPTER TWELVE

ISOBEL WENT HOME.

The moment she arrived outside the house, however, it hit her that this wasn't her home at all. It was the home of Rafe and his boys. And that, despite everything that had happened since she'd first walked through this door, in this moment she felt about as welcome as she'd been the day of the funeral, when she'd shocked Rafe by turning up in his life again. For a long time Isobel stayed in her car, her thoughts swirling.

The shock of her reappearance seemed insignificant now, in comparison to the blow he'd just received. Isobel was feeling so torn in two herself that she buried her face in her hands. She wanted to be with Rafe. A large part of her desperately wanted to be as much of a rock for him in this rough patch as he'd been for her when Daisy had been hovering on the edge of survival. Surely he knew, deep down, that it made no difference to the relationship he had with his sons whether or not he was their biological father—in the same way that she couldn't love Daisy any more, whether or not she'd given birth to her?

But a larger part of Isobel knew that, as heartbreaking as it was, the last thing Rafe needed right now was to be in the company of Lauren Matthews' sister when it must seem as if she had managed to deliver an ultimate betrayal. This wasn't Isobel's fault and maybe Lauren had convinced herself that Rafe had fathered her twins, but it certainly wasn't Rafe's fault in any way, and it was totally unfair that he had to deal with this. He'd had one betrayal after another in his life, hadn't he? A father who'd rejected him as a baby, a wife who'd cheated on him, a woman who'd blackmailed him into marriage...

Had he now somehow linked letting Isobel back into his life with a worst-case scenario that his family was going to disintegrate?

Surely he'd see how wrong that was as soon as the initial shock of this news wore off?

But what was Isobel going to do in the meantime?

She couldn't stay out here in the car any longer. With a sigh that was almost a groan she went and let herself into the house.

Should she stay out of Rafe's way until he was ready to talk to her? Give him some time to feel safe with his boys in their own home? Until he could see her and not be reminded of the appalling secret her sister might have used to trap him and change his life for ever? Isobel could pack a bag and go to a hotel. She could even make the move into her childhood home in Barrington Street. The work on the house was by no means finished but it had been stripped and dried out enough to not be a health hazard. Lots of people managed to live in houses while renovations were happening around them.

But would her absence make things worse rather than better between her and Rafe? And she couldn't pack up and leave before explaining things to Oscar and Josh, could she? Had Rafe really been worried about the effect on his children of letting her back into his life? She would never intentionally do anything to hurt his boys. Or him, for that matter. You didn't do that to people you loved.

Absorbed in her thoughts, Isobel had walked

into her favourite room of this wonderful old home. She let Cheddar out into the garden and then put the kettle on, thinking that maybe a cup of strong coffee would help with the dark, foggy feeling in her head that made it impossible to know what the best thing to do was. Did Rafe need time alone with his boys to realise that nothing had really changed?

Or would it break any trust that had formed that she wasn't about to run away at the first sign of trouble?

There was no question of running away from this.

Because… Daisy… And Oscar. And Josh… And because… Rafe…

Isobel wasn't about to let her sister take away—for the second time—that dream of a future with the man she loved. It was more than worth fighting for. The only problem was that she had no idea how to begin that fight.

The kitchen was spotless, because she'd used the first anxious hours of waiting for news on Oscar last night to clean up the leftovers of the Mexican feast. Instead of opening a cupboard to find a clean mug for her coffee, Isobel opened the dishwasher. She could put these dishes away and use one of the clean mugs in there.

But when she pulled out a plate from the bottom rack, the feel of it in her hands made her head spin all over again.

It really felt as if someone was holding the other side of this plate.

No. Not someone. Rafe.

She could hear his voice.

'You were the one I loved, Belle. You were the one...'

Oh, help...

This wasn't helping clear her head at all. A scratch on the back door when Cheddar wanted to come back inside made Isobel wonder if being out in the garden would be better. And then she realised that she'd known the best place to go for some fresh air all along.

She'd just needed Cheddar to remind her.

It was early afternoon by the time Rafe got home with the boys.

He carried Oscar into the living room and found pillows and blankets to make him a bed on the couch.

'Just movies and games this afternoon,

okay? On the couch. You're going to need to be careful of your leg until it's all healed up.'

'Can I go to school?'

'Not until your leg's better. Josh will have to go back tomorrow but he can stay home with you this afternoon.'

'Will you stay home with me too?'

'Today I will, buddy. I'll get Helen to come and look after you tomorrow while I'm at work.'

'Aunty Belle could look after me.' Oscar's eyes were already drifting shut as he lay back against the pillows. Rafe tucked a blanket over him.

Josh looked up from where he was searching for a favourite movie on the shelf below the television. 'Where *is* Aunty Belle?'

'I don't know.'

'And where's Cheddar?' Oscar opened his eyes. 'I want him to come and sleep on the couch with me.'

'I don't know that either, buddy. Maybe he's out in the garden. I'll go and have a look for him.'

What Rafe *did* know was he needed to talk to Isobel. He'd had to focus on Oscar and being sure it was safe to take him home while he'd still been blindsided by the shocking discovery that he couldn't possibly be the twins' father but, in the back of his mind, waiting to surface, was the memory of how shocked Isobel had also been. The look in her eyes when words were leaking from what felt like a broken heart and he'd said that he wished he'd never met her sister.

A look that suggested she was hearing that he wished he'd never met *her*.

He didn't blame her for leaving the hospital. If he hadn't had his boys to care for, he might have done the same thing and gone to find a private place to think about what had happened and what it could mean but, in a way, having to keep them entertained and out of trouble, reassure Josh that his brother was going to be absolutely fine and pretend that hamburgers and French fries for a late breakfast was the best ever had been exactly what he'd needed to do in that initially stunned period.

Because it had allayed any fear that what he'd just found out could hurt his family in some way. It made it crystal clear that these boys were his. He'd taken responsibility for them before they were born, had loved them from the moment they'd taken their first breaths and would protect and support them in any way he could until *he* took his last breath. Whether or not he'd actually fathered them didn't matter a damn. Any more than it mattered that Isobel hadn't given birth to Daisy. She *was* that baby's mother. Rafe had known that since he'd seen her that first time, with the precious infant against her bare skin. When he'd seen the love in her eyes when she'd made the decision to adopt Daisy and the courage with which she'd stepped up to take on that enormous responsibility.

The kitchen and the garden felt empty enough to let him know instantly that Cheddar wasn't anywhere to be found in or around the house. That Isobel wasn't either. And it felt as if Rafe had actually swallowed that empty feeling because it was lodged in his gut. In a Belle-shaped kind of hole. It wasn't until he came back inside that Rafe saw the note on the table, near the school books that weren't going to be needed today. He took it back to the living room.

'Aunty Belle's taken Cheddar for a walk. She's left you guys a note.'

'What does it say?'

'Um…' Rafe cleared his throat. 'It says… um…' The words on the note were blurring slightly and he had to blink.

Josh took the slip of paper from his hand. 'Let *me* read it, Daddy. I'm good at reading now.'

'Me too.' Oscar was pushing himself up-right on his pillows and Josh wriggled onto the couch so they could both look at Isobel's clear printing.

'Dear Oscar and Josh. I'm taking Ched-dar for a walk…because I want to find a… What's that word, Daddy?'

'Special.'

'And that one?'

'Bead.'

'A *special* bead stone for Oscar because he's got a sore leg.'

The boys were taking turns to read each line.

'And one for Josh because I know how scary it is to have something bad happen to someone you love. You're both very…what's that word, Daddy?'

'Brave.'

'Lots of love from Aunty Belle.'

Oscar and Josh looked at each other.

'I love Aunty Belle,' Josh said.

'Me too.' Oscar nodded.

'Daddy?' Josh was looking very serious. 'Do you love Aunty Belle?'

Rafe had to try and swallow the huge lump in his throat. 'Yeah…' He had to blink again too. 'I really do.'

Cheddar had given up chasing seagulls.

Isobel had found what she'd been searching for. The two special stones but, more importantly, a clear head and a calmness that came with certainty. It was probably past time she went home but she hadn't wanted to move. The sunshine was warm enough today for the sea breeze to be a delight and the wash of gentle waves on the pebbles was a balm to her soul. But she was ready now and she pushed herself to her feet.

She'd been sitting just below the point where the stony shore started sloping towards the sea so it wasn't until she stood up that she saw another person on the beach. The figure was too far away for her to recognise but she knew who it was.

Rafe…

Pebbles crunched and slid beneath her feet

as she tried to walk faster. Cheddar bounded ahead and then ran in figures-of-eight between them as they got closer. And closer. Close enough to both reach out at exactly the same time to hold each other tightly enough to suggest that neither of them ever wanted to let the other go. Except they did, of course. Just far enough to kiss each other. And then kiss each other again.

And then they both sat on the stones and held hands just as tightly as they'd held each other and Cheddar lay down with a resigned sigh because no one was paying him the slightest attention.

'I *was* coming home,' Isobel told Rafe.

'I know. But I couldn't wait. And there are two little boys who want to see you.' Rafe was smiling. 'Helen told me to take as long as it took, though. I think she knew how important this was.'

'You coming to find me?'

'No.' Rafe leaned in to kiss her again. 'I've already done that. I found you and I fell in love with you. Again. Or maybe I still was even after all these years. This was about not losing you.'

'Not possible.' Isobel caught her bottom lip

between her teeth. 'I could go to the other side of the world again but I'd be leaving most of me here. With you. Important bits—like my heart. I know that because I've already done it and I don't want to do it again.'

'I don't want you to do it again. I want all of you here. I'm happy to share, with Oscar and Josh and Daisy but...you know what?'

Isobel's smile felt misty. 'What?'

'The house felt so empty when we got home and you weren't there. My life would feel even emptier without you.'

Isobel was blinking back tears now. 'I love you. It's only ever been you, Rafe. Like someone wise once told me, when you know, you know.'

Rafe was blinking too. 'Very wise, that person. When I stopped being scared this morning I realised that I know I'm a father. Nothing can change that. And I know how much I need *you*. How much I love you. Nothing's going to change that either.'

There was only the sound of the wash of waves on pebbles for a long, long moment as Isobel let herself fall into the love she could see in Rafe's eyes. It really was time to go home now. Because it really *was* home she would be going to. She remembered to pick up the stones she'd spent so long searching for.

'Can I see?' Rafe reached for one of the stones—an especially smooth, flat, round white stone with a perfect hole right in the centre. 'Wow...this is a beauty.'

'I like this one too.' Isobel held onto the hollow tube of grey stone that was lined with white.

They both held their stones up to their eyes.

'What can you see?' Isobel asked softly, even though she knew perfectly well that Rafe could only see her.

'A magic place,' Rafe told her. 'I can see into the future.'

Isobel could see his smile through the hole in her stone. 'How 'bout that?' she murmured. 'I can see exactly the same thing.'

EPILOGUE

Nearly three years later...

'I'VE GOT SOMETHING to tell you.'

'I think I already know.' Rafe was standing beneath the biggest tree in the garden, a magnificent old oak that had a branch strong enough for a swing made out of rope and an old tractor tyre.

'Really? But I only just found out myself. Like, a minute ago.'

Isobel kept walking until she was so close to Rafe her body was touching his. And then she leaned a little closer, pushing him back against the trunk of the tree, and tilted her head up in an invitation to be kissed.

'Daisy told me.' Rafe accepted the invitation and kissed her with a thoroughness that made her toes curl.

'Oh… Really? I wonder how she knows?'

Isobel turned her head at the sound of barking. Their new puppy, Brie, was trying to entice Cheddar to play but the older dog was simply sitting there like a golden rock, wagging his tail. Brie gave up and bounced towards where Oscar and Josh were kicking a football around on the lawn, knocking Daisy off her feet as she went past her. Daisy shrieked with laughter, got up and also joined the game of football.

'She's about to turn three, that girl of ours. She knows everything.'

Isobel laughed. 'And she's so bossy.'

'Yep.' Rafe was grinning. 'I'd tell you what she said but I think it's supposed to be a secret.'

He lifted a hand to touch one of the strings hanging from another branch of this old tree. A string with stones knotted down its length. There were three of them now. Daisy had been helping to find bead stones since she began walking. Before that even, when they sat on the beach for a picnic and she would sit there, having invented the game of holding up every stone she could fit into her little hand to find out if it had a hole in it or not.

Isobel merely raised her eyebrows and

Rafe's grin widened. 'Okay, okay…she told me that she was going to have a pirate party for her birthday.'

'I wonder whose idea that really was?'

'I know. Oscar's still telling everyone he's a real pirate and he's got the scar to prove it.'

'I don't mind doing a pirate party, if that's what she wants. And it probably is, because she loves everything her big brothers love. We won't do the boat, though.'

'No.' Rafe's agreement was heartfelt. 'Or plastic swords.'

'That wasn't what I came out here to tell you, though.'

'Oh?' Rafe was watching Isobel's face and maybe there was something in her expression that gave him a clue. 'Oh, my God…' he breathed. 'You're not…?'

'Mmm. I am. I just did the test.'

Rafe pulled her into his arms, a bead stone string still tangled in his fingers. He was hugging her as tightly as he had that day he'd come to find her on the beach. The day they'd seen exactly this future through the holes in their stones.

'Okay, that does it,' Rafe finally said, his voice catching. 'We need to get married.'

Isobel laughed. 'I thought you'd never ask.'

'You mean you *want* to get married?'

Her smile faded. 'I've always wanted to marry you, Rafe. From the moment I met you.' Isobel stood on tiptoes to kiss him. 'But I knew you didn't want to do it again.'

'I want to now. When you know, you know.' He untangled the string from his fingers but, instead of letting it go, he caught one of the stones and held it up between them, so they could both see through the hole.

'What can you see?' he asked softly.

Isobel could see the man she loved through the frame of that hole. And behind him she could see three happy, healthy children and a couple of dogs playing in the evening sunshine. She could see the life she loved with all her heart. The family she loved so much that sometimes it hurt—in a very good way. And this family was growing in both size and strength. Isobel had to blink because the picture in that frame was getting a bit blurry now.

'Magic,' she whispered. 'That's what I can see.'

Rafe's voice was a whisper as well. 'Me too...'

* * * * *

If you enjoyed this story, check out these other great reads from Alison Roberts

**The Vet's Unexpected Family
Christmas Miracle at the Castle
Stolen Nights with the Single Dad
Unlocking the Rebel's Heart**

All available now!